Romance Allegro

Nydia Hadi

AOS Publishing, 2025
Copyright © 2025 Nydia Hadi

ISBN: 978-1-998662-19-7

Cover Design: Jessica James

Visit AOS Publishing's website:
www.aospublishing.com

Chapter 1

Early October
Downtown Toronto

"So, what are we going to do after this?" Erica asks.

Raphael Zhang knows that she is waiting for further invitation to his apartment. They met online a few weeks ago and today is the first time they meet each other in person. Erica is a gorgeous-looking Asian girl. She is twenty-four years old, a bit too young for him, who is thirty years old. They have just had a fun dinner at one of the Japanese restaurants downtown. However, he doesn't have any plan to continue meeting her. There is nothing wrong with her. He is just not interested.

"I have to see my friends after this," Raphael says.

"At this hour? It's almost nine p.m."

"Yes." He is not lying. Today is Friday and he is going to have a movie night and sleepover at Gaby's place. Gaby is his younger sister. She is currently living with André, her fiancé, at Shangri-La. Their place has three bedrooms. His other younger sister, Michelle, and her boyfriend, Guillaume, will also join them for the movie night and sleepover.

These movie nights and sleepovers are kind of their monthly or bi-weekly routines. The last time they did this, André told him that he can bring a girl if he wants. As much as Raphael wants, there is no girl he considers bringing into his close circle at this point. At least not yet.

"Okay. When will we see each other again?" Erica asks.

"I will text you," Raphael lies.

"Okay." Erica seems disappointed. She probably has enough dating experience to know that this is a common line a guy uses if he is not interested in meeting you further.

After saying goodbye to Erica, Raphael walks towards Shangri-La. It takes him only ten minutes. At nine p.m, Toronto is still busy, especially on Friday night: a lot of noises coming from the bars and a lot of nicely-dressed young people pass by the street.

Once in front of the Shangri-La Residence, he presses the buzzer, and it's either Gaby or André who lets him in from the phone. He passes the lobby and concierge and walks towards the elevator. He has been very familiar with this luxurious building.

Gaby and André are living on the sixtieth floor. They moved here in May of this year. André used to live in Montreal. So did Guillaume. André and Guillaume have been best friends for six years before Raphael, Gaby, and Michelle met them. André used to be a concert pianist and Guillaume was his manager. Since both André and Guillaume are the only child, their relationship becomes more like brothers than just artist-manager.

Raphael, Gaby, and Michelle met André and Guillaume for the first time in Singapore during André's concert tour last December. It was Gaby's idea to follow André around the world to attend his concerts. Gaby has been a fan of André since she was a kid. During the tour in Singapore, André coincidentally heard her playing piano and invited her to perform on stage with him. It must have felt like a dream for Gaby to be invited to the stage by her idol. Then, she performed with André in Auckland, Geneva, and New York as well. After coming back from the tour, Gaby ended up enrolling in a music school to become a pianist like André. She used to be a CPA. When Gaby and André's relationship blossomed during the concert tour, Raphael automatically became friends too with André and Guillaume.

Not only André and Gaby, but Guillaume and Michelle also fell in love during the tour. Raphael thought this could only happen in the movies. Apparently, even one year later, Michelle and Guillaume's relationship remains strong. It was not just a fling during the trip. Gaby got engaged to André this August, and

Guillaume has been living with Michelle since he moved to Toronto last May.

Only Raphael hasn't been so lucky with love.

But he doesn't feel the peer pressure at all. He is not even sure if he is ready to date seriously or not. He is too busy working as an Emergency Medicine resident physician at the hospital. And he is busy with his own adventures. He hasn't found someone who is as adventurous as him.

He particularly likes extreme sports like skiing, mountain climbing, and skydiving. When he told girls about this, they looked at him with horror. Some looked at him with admiration, but it was clear to him that they were not interested in doing this type of adventure themselves. Today, it was even more boring with Erica. She was only interested in his life as a doctor, but she didn't seem to be interested in his adventures at all.

Finally, the elevator arrives at the sixtieth floor. He walks towards André's unit and knocks.

Gaby opens the door right away. "Raphael! Come in!" she says excitedly. But her excitement doesn't last long when she realizes that he is coming by himself.

"Oh, you don't invite the girl?" she asks while letting him in.

"Nope. I hope you are not disappointed," he says.

"I'm not. But I hope you are not."

"I am relieved that I am free from her now."

"Oh." Gaby seems like she doesn't know what to say.

They walk towards the high-ceiling and spacious living room with a view of Toronto downtown night skylines.

"Hey Raphael. How are you doing?" André appears in the living room. Raphael examines his face automatically. He will always be worried about André's health. Last year, André had an open-heart surgery due to his congenital heart problem that led to serious complications during his concert tour. He even went into cardiac arrest on the stage when performing in New York and Raphael had to resuscitate him. It still traumatized Raphael now.

Although he has seen worse cases in the ER, it still feels different when someone who collapses in front of you is someone you know, or worse, your future brother-in-law.

Luckily, André has beaten the odds and survives. But there are still possibilities that he may experience complications after the surgery.

"I am good. How are you?" Raphael replies.

"Good! So, it didn't work out with this girl?" André asks while Raphael is taking off his jacket.

"No. I think I may take a break from dating," he says, and sits on the couch. He is very tired today. He had a twelve-hour shift in the hospital before meeting Erica.

"You always say that."

"Do I?" He doesn't even realize.

"Yeah. Just take it easy, Raphael. Don't force it but still be open to it," André suggests.

Raphael always liked André. Although André is a few months younger than him, Raphael feels like André is more mature and wiser than him. He always thinks of André as his own brother. Raphael is also very close to Guillaume, who is a year older than both of them. But there is still a cultural barrier between him and Guillaume sometimes, as Guillaume is Caucasian and from Quebec. Raphael himself is Canadian-born Asian. His parents are from Hong-Kong. There are things that he experienced as a first-generation Asian-Canadian that Guillaume wouldn't be able to relate to. André can still relate to some extent because he is mixed-race. André's dad was French-Canadian like Guillaume, but his mother was Korean. Unfortunately, both André's parents passed away in a car accident seven years ago. Maybe the stress of losing them also contributed to rapid deterioration of André's heart condition before his surgery last year.

Although Raphael, André, and Guillaume are not the same race, they get along very well. The three of them are attractive in their own ways. Every time they walk together in downtown

Toronto, people always stare at them. Guillaume has blonde hair and blue eyes. He is tall and muscular. André has brown hair, small Asian eyes, and a sharp Caucasian nose. He is tall and lean, too, although he has lost a bit of weight after his surgery. Raphael has typical black hair and Asian facial features. He also wears glasses because he has read a lot of science books since he was a kid. Raphael is also tall and muscular for Asian standards, and this is thanks to his sporty nature. He plays tennis and squash in addition to his adventures. Many people think he looks like Hyun Bin, one of the most handsome Korean actors, although it is André who has Korean blood.

"Guillaume and Michelle haven't come yet?" Raphael changes topics. He doesn't want to talk about his love life, because it is nonexistent.

"They will arrive soon," André says.

Right after André says that, his phone rings, and it is the buzzer from the front door. He lets them in, and not long after, Guillaume and Michelle appear in front of his suite.

"Hey guys!" Michelle greets them excitedly. Michelle is always the life of the party. She is the youngest at twenty-four years old, and is the most energetic and extroverted. Raphael considers himself an extrovert, too, but Michelle is one level above him. They sometimes cannot stop arguing. Although Michelle is two years younger than Gaby, Michelle is mentally stronger than Gaby and more confident. Maybe because she is a ballet dancer, while Gaby is more sensitive and insecure. That's why Raphael naturally feels more protective towards Gaby, even though he loves them both. And Raphael is relieved that Gaby has found André and Michelle has found Guillaume.

Guillaume kisses Gaby on both cheeks to greet her while André kisses Michelle. Raphael is still not used to this Quebec/French culture thing.

"Hey, there you are, Raphael! How are you?" Guillaume greets him.

"Stop there, Guillaume. Don't kiss me," Raphael says.

"Yuck, I won't. You are a man."

"I'm good. How are you?"

"Good. Where is the girl? Did you bring her?"

"What girl? There is no girl," he says.

Michelle jumps in, "What happened this time, Raphael? Did you break her heart again?" She says with a teasing tone.

"No, I didn't. I was just not interested."

Guillaume shakes his head, "Oh, my God. I am worried that you will only find a girl when you are fifty," When Raphael met Guillaume the first time, he remembered that Guillaume was a quiet guy like André. Now it seems like he has become more outgoing and chattier after meeting Michelle.

Luckily André steps in, "Stop teasing him guys. What are we going to watch, by the way?" André asks. Raphael is relieved.

"*The Exorcist!* The 1973 film," Michelle replies enthusiastically.

Raphael almost drops his glass. "What? No way."

"What's wrong with you, Raphael? I thought you were an adrenaline junkie. This is a perfect movie for you," Michelle says.

"This movie is not good for André. What if he has a heart attack?" Raphael says.

"Hey, don't use me to avoid watching horror movies," André says while laughing. "Let's vote. Who agrees to watch this tonight?" André asks. He raises his hand himself. Michelle, Guillaume, and Gaby also raise their hands. Even Gaby!

"You too, Gabs? Really?" He almost feels betrayed.

"Yes. C'mon, Raphael. It's gonna be fun. We are going to turn off all the lights and watch in the dark," Gaby says.

Although he likes adrenaline, watching horror movies is never his favorite. Maybe because he has seen deaths in the hospital and he feels like ghosts are real.

"Are you guys sure? I have seen enough horror in the ER, you know," he says.

But they insist, so he has no choice but to follow them. They all sit in the living room with blankets, snacks, and drinks.

Gaby rolls down a big projector by the giant floor-to-ceiling window. Now the projector covers the beautiful downtown Toronto view at night.

Raphael just takes a deep breath and braces himself.

Raphael is relieved when the movie is finally over. He only watched about half the scenes, and he didn't look at all during the scariest parts. Luckily the room was dark, so the others didn't notice that he didn't actually watch. There was a lot of blood and bodily fluids in the movie; he has seen enough of that in real life.

Everybody seemed to really enjoy the movie and cannot stop talking about it. He is actually surprised that André liked it, too. Even the movie is too hard for his heart. How did André manage?

Finally at around midnight, everybody is tired and they all say goodnight to each other. Raphael occupies the smaller bedroom on the second floor. Guillaume and Michelle are occupying the master bedroom on the second floor while André and Gaby sleep on the first-floor bedroom. André has settled in the first-floor bedroom since he bought this place because at that time, he was still recovering from his heart surgery, and climbing the stairs took effort for him.

Raphael is in the middle of enjoying the view of downtown Toronto at night from his bedroom when he hears a knock on his door. He quickly opens the door. Gaby is standing there.

"Can I come in?" Gaby asks.

"Of course." Raphael lets her in.

They lie down on the bed. Since they were kids, they liked to talk until late at night. Raphael always talks about his past and upcoming adventures to Gaby, even though Gaby herself is not adventurous at all. All she likes doing is studying and playing piano. But Gaby is such a good listener and Raphael likes to talk to her especially when he hasn't had any girlfriend with whom he can share his life. Gaby also always asks for his advice and opinion about her life problems. Raphael likes to solve problems.

"I hope you are not too sad that your date didn't work out again," Gaby says.

Raphael laughs. "You come here just to ask me about that? Don't worry, Gabs. It is the least of my concern. When I was with her today, I couldn't stop glancing at my watch. I was waiting for the time of our movie night. Although at the end the movie sucked."

"It was so good! So scary."

"Yeah, of course. I know why Michelle and you like watching horror movies. Because you can hug André whenever you are scared and Michelle can hug Guillaume."

"Err... You are partially right." Gaby blushes. "Anyway. I hope you find someone. I hope you don't feel left out because Michelle and I are in a relationship right now." Gaby always cares about how other people feel. She is very sensitive. It's her strength. That is what makes her a good musician. But there is a downside of it, too. She can be overly sensitive and think too much about what people think about her.

"I am not. Don't worry, Gabs. I am even happier that both you and Michelle have someone who can take care of you. And André and Guillaume are both good people. Although they come from a very different background than us, I really like them both. They both are extremely successful and more well-off than us, but they are very humble and not showing off," Raphael says.

"Yeah, me, too. And I can see that André and Guillaume really like you. They already consider you as their brother, too."

"Yeah, so do I."

"Okay then. If you feel alone, you can always talk to us or to Mom and Dad," Gaby says sympathetically.

"Thanks, Gab. But honestly, I am more excited in planning my next adventures than planning on dating."

"Yeah? What's the next adventure you have in mind?"

"I want to go hiking in the Rocky Mountains next summer. Maybe somewhere in Lake Louise or Kananaskis. Last time, I hiked Mount Yamnuska in Kananaskis, and it was a legit hike. We had to cross a ridge with a chain and we also had to scree ski on the way down."

"Stop it, Raphael. You always make Mom and I worry whenever you go mountain climbing, you know? You didn't have a phone signal. We couldn't reach you. I heard that there are a lot of bears there. And you sometimes hiked alone." Gaby sounds very worried.

"Don't worry, Gabs. I am a doctor, remember? I can take care of myself."

"But still. Can you just do regular stuff? Maybe we can watch a movie about people climbing Mount Everest and you can just imagine it was you."

"It's not the same, Gabs. Anyway, how is it going between you and André?" Raphael tries to change topics.

Gaby sighs. "It's okay. I think he is recovering well physically. And I am very relieved about that. However, I notice that he seems very depressed and anxious sometimes, even though he tries to appear normal in front of me," Gaby says.

Raphael doesn't answer at first. He knows that depression and anxiety are common after a heart surgery.

"Of course, we cannot deny that his life is not going to be the same anymore, right?"

"Yeah, but regardless, we are still forever grateful to you, Raphael. If it wasn't because of you, he wouldn't be here. I wouldn't have such a kind and caring fiancé like André." Gaby hugs him, Raphael hugs her back. The bond between André, Gaby, and him is stronger since he saved André's life. Even with Guillaume and Michelle as well. Guillaume is still protective towards André, too, even though he is no longer André's manager.

After Gaby leaves, Raphael finds it hard to fall asleep. Because he cares about André, it's hard not to think about his health. Depression and anxiety? Psychology and psychiatry are never his forte. He is more worried if André has physical symptoms like new chest pain or arrhythmia. He just hopes that André's family doctor or cardiologist knows what they are doing.

Chapter 2

Early October
Downtown Toronto

Stephanie Adams wakes up at exactly six o'clock every morning. Today is no exception. After splashing cold water onto her face, she puts on her gym clothes, which are a black sports bra and tight legging pants. Then she hits the gym on the tenth floor of her apartment building. Going to the gym has been her daily morning routine.

There are not many people at the gym at six a.m. She runs on the treadmill for fifteen minutes to warm up. While running on the treadmill, she can enjoy Toronto's downtown view from the tenth floor. She lives in the downtown area near College Station. She likes that it is very convenient to go everywhere. It is still dark outside at six a.m. in October. While running on the treadmill, she is listening to K-pop music.

She started taking interest in K-pop music when she was in university. For her, the music feels very foreign to her. She likes everything that is exotic and unfamiliar. Since then, she has been learning Korean. Now at twenty-eight years old, she can speak and understand Korean fluently. She can even sing, rap, and dance to some K-pop music.

Stephanie is a certified music therapist. She has been doing music therapy for four years since she graduated with her Master's in music therapy. For her, music therapy is not a job. It's a calling. It's something she is passionate about. It allows her to use music to help people with various psychological and physical needs. Sometimes, she incorporated K-pop music to her Korean or Asian clients who can relate to the music. Aside from K-pop music and dance, she is also a classical violinist. With the broad approach of music therapy, her proficiency in K-pop music, dance, and classical violin really make her a well-rounded music therapist.

After the treadmill, she does some deadlifts, squats, bench press, and abdominal exercise. Maybe it's just her nature to be interested in anything that involves physical activities. That is shown in her toned body. For a woman, Stephanie is extremely muscular. It doesn't even take effort for her to build muscle. She always feels the compulsion to move her body, like dancing or doing sports. She cannot just sit around and do nothing.

After she is done with weightlifting, she does some High Intensity Interval Training. This is another exercise routine that she likes. No wonder the last time she checked; her body fat was only twenty percent. At the end of her exercise, she looks at herself in the mirror.

People always say that she is beautiful in her own way. She has dark brown hair and pale skin. What stands out from her appearance are definitely her broad shoulders and muscular arms, due to her regular swimming exercise. Unfortunately, her chest is almost flat. She has a small waist but straight hips and legs. So, her body is more like an apple shape and more like a man. In the past, she used to be insecure about this. But now, she just embraces it. She would not stop working out or stop doing activities that she likes just because she is afraid of being more muscular than necessary. Everybody says that she is a tomboy and she should be more feminine. But she just wants to be herself.

Her love life is almost non-existent. A lot of men only see her as a gym buddy or friend instead of as a romantic partner. Maybe because she always appears strong and independent. Even at twenty-eight years old, this doesn't bother her. She enjoys being single. Even if she ends up single for the rest of her life, she doesn't mind. She is still interested in men, obviously. But unfortunately, she never really falls in love.

After the gym, she goes back to her apartment unit on the twenty-fourth floor to eat breakfast, shower, and get ready. She has two appointments booked for today. The first is a private appointment with Emery Carlson, a six-year-old child with ASD (Autistic Spectrum Disorder) who requires music therapy intervention to improve his communication skills and emotional regulation; the second appointment is for Helen McKenzie, a seventy-five-year-old lady with Alzheimer's.

It doesn't take her long to dress up. She always wears a blouse and jeans. Her parents and her friends always complain that she should dress more feminine, like by wearing a dress. But she almost never wears a dress. She likes wearing a blouse because it accentuates her broad shoulders. She feels confident about it regardless of what people think.

At eight-thirty a.m., she leaves her place and drives to Emery's house in Davisville Village.

Stephanie is satisfied with her session with Emery. Today they did an improvisational therapy. She let Emery use maracas and tambourines. In the beginning, they made a rhythm together, and after that she started to sing a simple song that fit into that rhythm while Emery followed along. At the end she stopped and Emery continued on his own. That's considered a huge progress. They also made more eye contact throughout the session.

Stephanie thinks the day couldn't go better than this. Unfortunately, she concludes too fast. When she enters the living room with Emery, Emery's mom, Anabelle, is there talking on the phone and laughing. At the same time, a fire truck passes by and causes a loud noise. The television in the living room is also running. All these noises seem to be overwhelming for Emery. He starts to become agitated. Anabelle pauses talking on the phone and looks at Stephanie with a helpless look.

"What's wrong with him, Stephanie?" Anabelle asks while covering her cell phone speaker with her hand. Her eyes look worried. Meanwhile, Emery starts throwing anything he can get his hands on. Plates, glasses, framed photos, ornaments, vases, et cetera. Now everything becomes uncontrollable. All the broken glass is now scattered on the floor. The environment becomes extremely hazardous.

"It's the noise, Anabelle." Stephanie tries not to panic. "Let's get him out of here."

Before they can do anything, Emery seems to stumble and is going to fall exactly on the broken glass on the floor.

Without thinking Stephanie uses her athletic body to prevent Emery from falling. She falls to the ground first on her arms before grabbing Emery's body with her other free arm. After that, Anabelle quickly grabs Emery away from the broken glass on the floor.

"Oh my God, are you okay, Stephanie?" Anabelle's face is full of horror while looking at Stephanie on the floor on top of the broken glasses.

"Yes, yes. Get him out of here quickly!" Stephanie is panting.

She sighs with relief once Anabelle and Emery are out of sight. But now she knows that she has a bigger problem. She looks at her right arm; it's all covered with blood from the wrist until the elbow.

Thirty minutes later, she is waiting in one of the exam rooms in the emergency department in one of the hospitals downtown. Earlier, she drove herself from Emery's place to the ER despite the bleeding from the cuts on her arm. It stings but she still can bear it. She is used to injury due to her sporty nature. Most of them were sprains. Also, she is used to being pulled on the hair or being hit or kicked by some disabled kids. But so far, this is the most serious injury she has had while on the job. By the time she arrived at the ER, the nurse looked at her arm in horror and quickly took her vital signs and put her under category-three triage. In less than ten minutes, she was directed to a room and a nurse carefully helped her into a gown. Now she is waiting for the doctor to see her and probably suture the wound. 'It's going to heal well eventually,' she thinks while looking at her wounded arm.

Suddenly, someone opens the curtain of her room. Her heart almost stops when she sees a handsome man standing there. Wow. He looks like one of the Korean men in the K-pop boy band that she listened to this morning. Only he appears more fit and muscular than them, it's still obvious even though he is wearing scrubs. He also appears very capable and smart behind his glasses.

"Good morning, Ms. Adams. My name is Raphael Zhang. I am a resident physician here and I will be helping you today," the guy says with a friendly but confident and professional tone.

Throughout her life, Stephanie only has a few Asian male friends. Usually, they are more shy than her Caucasian male friends. But this Raphael Zhang is different. He is definitely charming and confident. He looks very exotic, especially his eyes, although they are behind the glasses. However, from the way he speaks, Stephanie guesses that this guy was probably born here because he doesn't have any accent.

"Hi... Raphael? Or should I call you Dr. Zhang? Umm. Thanks. I am Stephanie." She is suddenly nervous. Normally, she doesn't get nervous easily in front of a guy. She is usually confident, but not in front of this guy.

"You can call me Raphael." He smiles and takes a seat, and starts examining her wounded arm. When he touches her arms, she feels her heart flutter again, although he is wearing gloves. She suddenly feels very underdressed with a hospital gown. At least she is still wearing her jeans.

"This looks very bad. You are going to need several stitches," he says. "Are you right-handed or left-handed?"

"Left-handed. Thank God."

"Do you have any allergies to medications?"

"No."

"Great. I will be back." He gets up and exits the room. Once Raphael is outside, Stephanie realizes that she is holding her breath.

Raphael comes back with a nurse who brings several medical instruments that look like surgical instruments. The nurse puts a gown on him, and she starts putting an IV on Stephanie's uninjured arm and administering a local anesthetic to numb her arm as per Raphael's instructions. Now Stephanie is lying down on the bed.

"How do you feel, Stephanie?" Raphael asks before continuing the procedure.

"I'm okay." She tries to appear calm.

"You are doing great so far." Raphael smiles again. Although he is now wearing a mask, Stephanie can imagine that handsome face when he smiles.

"I will start cleaning the wound and taking out the glass. It's better if you don't look," Raphael says.

"It's okay. I prefer to look," Stephanie says. She is not scared of these things at all. And by looking at what he is going to do, she feels that she has more control.

"Okay then. Ready?" Raphael asks. She nods.

Raphael does everything very efficiently and quickly, but still very carefully and gently. It appears like he knows exactly what he is doing. There is no hesitation at all. Stephanie is impressed. In the beginning, she is curious to see what he is doing with her arm, but overtime her neck is tired and she just faces the ceiling and closes her eyes. She almost falls asleep until she hears Raphael starts talking.

"So, per your triage notes, you were with an autistic kid who suddenly became violent and started breaking things, and then you got injured while trying to prevent him from falling to the ground full of broken glass?" Raphael asks while suturing her wounds.

"Yes."

"That's very brave of you."

"Thank you."

"What is your job again?"

"I am a music therapist."

"Oh." Raphael doesn't say anything further. She knows right away that he is someone who doesn't believe in music therapy. A lot of medical professionals don't believe in it, either. Stephanie feels a bit disappointed. But why does she even care about Raphael's opinion?

"What instrument do you play?" Raphael asks. This is another common misconception. People usually think that music therapy is solely passive listening. They think the music therapist will play his or her instrument, and the client will just listen passively.

"I play the violin. And singing, too, sometimes."

"That's very cool. My sister is currently studying to become a pianist. She plays the piano really well," Raphael says. He seems really proud when talking about his sister. So, on top of being a capable doctor, he is also a caring brother.

"Nice." Stephanie doesn't know what else to say. But she feels like she wants to share more about music therapy. It is her passion. Her life. She wishes many people would be more appreciative towards it.

"You know, music therapy is not just listening to therapists playing their instruments. It's more than that. We have several methods, not just receptive therapy. There is improvisational therapy, rhythm therapy, and many more depending on the needs of the clients. We sometimes get them to actively play the musical instrument, or sing, or even compose a song. For some people, music therapy is really beneficial. It can help with emotional regulations, communications, pain management, and even motor skills..." Then Stephanie realizes that she may have talked too much. Why does she think that she has to justify her profession to Raphael?

"So, the kid who caused this injury, were you treating him with music therapy?" Raphael asks.

"Yes, we made so much progress today. He made more eye contact and he was more independent. He can even sing on his own," Stephanie says proudly.

"Then why was he still breaking things and making you end up here?" Raphael asks. His tone is actually not a mocking tone, but it does sound like he challenged her. She doesn't like it.

"Are all your patients always cured in one treatment session?" She challenges him back.

"How many sessions have you had with this kid?" Raphael ignores her question.

Now she starts to dislike this guy. Yes, he is definitely cocky and a bit disrespectful. She initially thought that he was a charming but humble guy. It turns out that he is just like a typical guy that she despises. Overconfident, thinking they are so good, and they are aware of their good looks and thus treating others as they like.

"I have been seeing him for a year. But you know how ASD is. Even with medications, you cannot just treat ASD in a year. But you can certainly improve their lives in many ways." Stephanie cannot hold herself back anymore. She should not continue debating with Raphael while her arm is at his mercy like this. Fortunately, Raphael is very professional. He doesn't change the pace of his suturing just because they got into an argument.

"For sure. I hope your treatment is working well for him," Raphael says. She cannot really tell if this is sarcasm or a genuine comment. She decided to just dismiss it. She cannot wait to get out of this room and forget about this cocky guy.

After that, Raphael continues his treatment in silence. Maybe he realizes that she is a bit offended. But at least he is still being thorough in his care. He bandages her stitched wounds gently and he gives her a tetanus shot just in case. He also prescribes a painkiller. It's a bit awkward after their small argument but overall, he is still kind.

"Please keep your wound dry for at least twenty-four hours. Also, avoid any strenuous exercise until it fully heals. Don't swim and don't sweat," Raphael says. How does he know that she likes to swim and sweat out in the gym?

"Also, you need to come back here in about ten to fourteen days from now to remove the stitches. You will be contacted to schedule an appointment and I will meet you at the clinic so that you don't have to come to the ER. However, come back here right away if your wound gets infected or you start having a fever, okay?" He looks at her while giving her the discharge notes. Now he is no longer wearing a mask so she can see his friendly face again. But it's too late. She has seen a part of his personality that she doesn't like already.

She nods, mutters thanks, and then leaves. Although she is not satisfied with the doctor, at least she is satisfied with the treatment.

Chapter 3

Mid-October
Downtown Toronto

Raphael and Guillaume are in the middle of doing a squash rally in Court 1. They both are good at this sport in different ways. Guillaume can hit the little black ball with full power until the ball sometimes bounces back to the glass door behind them, while Raphael can move across the court faster as he is lighter than Guillaume. Their rally is incredible until people gather outside of their court to watch their match.

At the end of the match, Guillaume wins by a slight margin. Raphael is a bit disappointed but he acknowledges that it was a fun game. He also justifies his loss with the excuse that he was tired after doing a twelve-hour shift that he has just finished two hours earlier. Although, even without the twelve-hour shift, he usually still lost against Guillaume.

"Good match, man," Guillaume says while drinking his water.

"Agreed," Raphael says half-heartedly. He is also drinking his water and wipes the sweat on his forehead and neck with the towel.

"Are you sure you still want to come to André's place tonight? You look like you are about to pass out after our last match," Guillaume says.

"Of course I will still come. I have a day off tomorrow," Raphael says.

They are about to leave, as they only booked the court for one hour.

But then Raphael sees a familiar face walking towards their direction to Court 1.

It's Stephanie.

Raphael almost chokes on his water. What is she doing here? She is not going to play squash while she still has stitches on her arm, is she? She will have an appointment with him tomorrow to remove the stitch.

Stephanie also freezes when she sees Raphael. It appears that she recognizes him, too.

Raphael cannot deny that Stephanie looks very attractive in her squash outfit. She wears a sleeveless top and shorts. The outfit really accentuates her broad shoulders and strong legs. Last time when she wore a hospital gown, even Raphael could tell that she is extremely muscular for a woman. That's why he was surprised when she said that she was a music therapist. He thought that she must be an athlete or personal trainer at least. Now with her workout clothes, her arms and legs muscles are visible. Wow.

Although Raphael's type is more feminine, he still finds her very attractive. Also, for the past few days, he realized that he couldn't get her out of his head. Normally, Raphael didn't pay much attention to his patients after he finished treating them. But Stephanie is too unique to be forgotten. More than a week ago, she showed up in the ER with a bloody arm full of broken glass, but she appeared very calm. She even drove herself to the ER. And when he stitched her arm, she didn't even flinch. Raphael found her very brave and impressive. Unfortunately, when they got into a discussion about music therapy, she seemed offended. At that time, he was purely curious about music therapy. He asked her questions out of curiosity and not for the purpose of doubting her skills. But Gaby and Michelle have told him multiple times that he sometimes comes across too bluntly and it can be rude and insulting for some people.

Stephanie nods at him but continues to walk towards the court.

"Stephanie?" Raphael decides to stop her.

She turns to him. "Yes?"

"What are you doing here?" he asks.

"I am about to play squash, obviously," she says in a flat tone.

"With your injured arm? What did I tell you about avoiding strenuous exercise?" Raphael realizes that he may come across as rude again.

"It's healing fine now. Thanks for your concern." She turns to the squash court.

"Wait." Raphael grabs her uninjured left arm. Stephanie looks a bit surprised. Raphael quickly releases his grab on her arm.

"Sorry, I don't mean to interfere. But..." Raphael loses his words. He still feels like this girl is under his care even though they are now outside of the ER. At least until he removes the stitches and her arm is fully healed, he is not going to stay quiet when she is about to do strenuous exercise.

Guillaume, who is still there, seems to feel a bit of tension between them. And he can guess that she is probably his patient.

"Raphael, let her play," Guillaume says with a friendly smile. "Hi, Stephanie. Sorry about my friend. He is too dedicated to his job. Anyway, are you playing with someone tonight?" Guillaume asks.

Stephanie turns to Guillaume and replies, "Unfortunately, my friend canceled at the last minute. Since we already booked the court, I decided to just play by myself."

"Oh, can I join you instead? Raphael and I have been playing for an hour. He is already tired, while I still have some energy," Guillaume says. Raphael looks at Guillaume in disbelief. Didn't he hear that Stephanie cannot play squash with her injured arm?

"Sure," Stephanie says.

Then Guillaume and Stephanie walk into the court and start doing a warmup rally, leaving Raphael outside of the court by himself. Seriously, Guillaume? What is he doing with this girl? Is he flirting with her while he is dating Michelle? Raphael is almost frustrated.

He is even more frustrated when he sees that Stephanie is almost as good as Guillaume at squash. At the end of the match, Guillaume only won by one point, and even after they prolonged the game because they tied. They look like they had a lot of fun.

Raphael is now very frustrated. Not only was this girl dismissing his order, but she is also better than him at squash. He decides that he cannot bear looking at them anymore and he walks towards the changing room to shower.

Once he finishes showering, he finds that Guillaume and Stephanie have just finished their second match. Guillaume sees him coming towards them and he says, "By the way, Raphael, I have just invited Stephanie to André's place tonight. I hope you don't mind. I think it will be fun."

What? Raphael looks at Stephanie. Now she is sweating and her face is red, which makes her even sexier. Wait, what is he thinking?

Stephanie's face looks livelier after playing squash with Guillaume. He hopes that Stephanie doesn't have a crush on Guillaume. Raphael doesn't know if it's because Guillaume is dating Michelle or because Raphael himself is starting to have a crush on Stephanie. No way. He wouldn't have a crush on this girl. She is not his type, is she?

Before Raphael can say anything, Guillaume leaves to the changing room, and so does Stephanie.

André looks excited when he welcomes Stephanie. Gaby and Michelle also look super enthusiastic. They think that Stephanie is here as Raphael's "guest".

Raphael pulls Guillaume aside as soon as they arrive at André's place.

"Guillaume, what are you thinking? Why did you invite Stephanie here? You are dating Michelle for God's sake." Raphael almost cannot hide his frustration.

"Wow, wow. Chill, man. I am not interested in Stephanie that way. I am doing this for you, Raphael. You are into this girl, right?" Guillaume asks.

"What? No way. She is not my type."

"Oh. Okay." Guillaume is a bit disappointed.

"You should not have invited her here. Now what will she think?"

"Well, regardless of whether you decide to pursue her or not, she can be a great squash partner or gym buddy for me. Or for us. She is the coolest girl I have ever met. You should admit it Raphael, she is slightly stronger than you," Guillaume says with a teasing smile and then leaves to join the crowd.

It turns out that it's not only Guillaume who gets along very well with Stephanie. Even André, Gaby, and Michelle seem to be fascinated by her. Initially, Raphael doesn't understand. How come this girl manages to charm everybody?

Raphael starts to see a different side of Stephanie. She is now looking very happy and shining among his close circle. Yes, his close circle. She is talking a lot and full of enthusiasm. It's very different from when she was interacting with him. While the rest of the group gathers on the couch, Raphael is sitting at the bar not far from the couch. He can still follow the conversation and see what's going on.

"So do you speak Korean at all?" Stephanie asks André after she discovers that he is half-Korean, half-Canadian.

"Yes, I do speak Korean," André says.

Then Stephanie asks André something in Korean. André's jaw drops. Not only André, but also everybody in the room including Raphael. André replies in Korean and they start conversing back and forth in Korean. Everybody is just so impressed. When a Caucasian girl speaks Korean, it's very uncommon. Stephanie keeps surprising him. What other hidden talent that she has that he doesn't know?

"So how come you speak Korean so well?" André asks. He is clearly impressed.

"I am always fascinated about Korean culture. I went to South Korea multiple times. I watch a lot of Korean dramas. And I am a big fan of K-pop," Stephanie replies.

Now it's Gaby and Michelle's turn to be impressed. Raphael knows that his sisters are also a big fan of K-dramas and K-pop. Now the girls are very enthusiastic, talking about the latest K-dramas and K-pop bands. Raphael almost laughs when André and Guillaume don't look very enthusiastic when the girls start talking about some cool Korean actors and K-pop male singers. They join Raphael at the bar.

"So, how are you guys feeling when they are talking about their crushes on Korean actors and boy bands?" Raphael asks without hiding his smile. Especially to Guillaume.

"Well, I know that Gaby has a crush on some Korean actors, but hey, I am half-Korean. So, it only confirms that I am her type," André says confidently.

"I know that Michelle has a crush on some Korean actors and singers, but it's only a crush. For a romantic partner, I think her type is more like me," Guillaume also says confidently.

Raphael thinks that André and Guillaume are just trying to appear more confident than they actually are. For the first time, Raphael feels proud to be an Asian man, although he is not Korean. But most girls that he dated mistaken him as Korean. Wait, if Stephanie has a crush on Korean guys, does that mean that he is her type? Raphael starts to feel like a winner.

"Anyway, I am so glad that you met Stephanie. She is so cool. I can already see that you guys have the same interests," André says.

"Wait, you misunderstand. I didn't bring Stephanie here. It was Guillaume's idea. Today is only my second time meeting her," Raphael clarifies.

"Oh." André looks a bit disappointed.

Meanwhile the girls are still enthusiastically talking about Korean culture in the living room.

"Steph, you make me want to go to South Korea now. Let's go for Christmas break! What do you think?" Michelle says enthusiastically.

"Oh wow, that's a good idea, Michelle!" Gaby also sounds excited.

Stephanie doesn't answer at first. She looks hesitant for a second.

"What do you think, Steph? Do you want to join us?" Michelle asks Stephanie.

"Unfortunately, I will pass. I have been to Seoul so many times. In fact, I have booked a vacation to the neighboring country for this December."

"Neighboring country? You mean China? Or Japan?" Gaby asks.

"Actually, it's North Korea."

The room turns silent. Nobody says anything for a while. Everybody is looking at Stephanie, including the guys who are still sitting at the bar. Especially Raphael.

Raphael, André, and Guillaume decide to come back to the couch.

"Where are you going again, Stephanie?" André asks carefully.

"North Korea."

"Are we even allowed to go there?" Guillaume asks in disbelief.

"Yes, we can. If you are a US citizen or South Korean, it may be a bit more challenging, but for Canadian tourists, it should be pretty straightforward." Stephanie says.

"Why do you want to go there?" Gaby asks.

"I really want to see Korea from a different angle. And I see this trip as an adventure, too. I like going to places that are a bit dangerous and thrilling. I know that there is a risk I can get captured there. However, I have done my research, and the chance of being captured there is very low. As long as we don't do anything stupid," Stephanie says.

Michelle jumps in, "But I heard there are prison camps there. It's so scary, Steph."

"Yeah, I know this sounds crazy. But this is what I am looking for. And when I return to the west, I may appreciate our freedom more. And I probably would not see Canada in the same way again after visiting North Korea."

Everybody is silent again. They are still digesting what Stephanie said. This girl keeps surprising them with her unique perspective about everything.

Raphael cannot hide his curiosity, "How long are you going to be there?" It's the first time he finally speaks directly to Stephanie since they arrived.

"Only for five days. I will join a tour group and we will depart from Beijing, as there is no direct flight from here to Pyongyang."

Everybody is silent again.

"Anybody else is interested in going to North Korea?" Raphael asks the crowd.

It doesn't take one second for Michelle to answer, "I am sorry, Steph, but even if the trip is free, I still wouldn't go. I'm too scared," Michelle says.

"Yeah, me, too," Gaby adds.

Then, it's André's turn to make excuse, "Unfortunately, I am half-South Korean. I am sure the North Koreans wouldn't like it if they found out. Sorry, Steph,"

Guillaume also jumps in, "If I were Asian, I would probably be interested. But I am Caucasian. What if they mistook me as American?" He adds, which doesn't make sense at all because Stephanie herself is also Caucasian.

"It's okay, guys. I don't want you to come with me either. I know it's quite dangerous. It's risky. Don't feel bad. I will share my experience once I come back. If I come back," Stephanie says as if it's not a big deal if she doesn't come back.

Raphael finishes drinking his martini.

"You know what, Stephanie, I may be interested in joining you," Raphael says with a smile. Suddenly his adrenaline kicks in.

Chapter 4

Early December
Toronto – Beijing

Finally, the day that Stephanie has been waiting for has come. She will depart to the most mysterious place on Earth, North Korea. She is super nervous but excited.

Her arm has also healed well. Raphael has removed the stitches, and although the scar is still visible, it doesn't hurt anymore.

She admits that she has been thinking about Raphael a lot these past few weeks. This guy kept surprising her. She really enjoyed meeting his friends, André and Guillaume, as well as his sisters, Gabrielle and Michelle, the other day at André's place. Raphael seemed a bit distant at first because she dismissed his order not to do strenuous activities. But after hearing her plan of going to North Korea, Raphael's attitude changed one hundred and eighty degrees. He became extremely enthusiastic. Apparently, he likes doing adventurous and dangerous activities like her!

After that night, they exchanged phone numbers and he texted her often to make sure that they booked the same tour and the same flight to North Korea. Luckily his visa got approved very quickly. He also suggested that they got the appropriate vaccines. So last week they went to the clinic together and had a good time chatting about North Korea. She cannot forget the technician's face when he administered their vaccines. He was speechless when they mentioned that they were going to North Korea.

Stephanie thinks that as a friend, Raphael is not bad at all. She thinks that she has started to gain his respect. He, too, started to gain her respect. Although sometimes Raphael may seem blunt and sound like he knows it all, by now Stephanie realizes that he is just naturally a confident person, but not necessarily cocky as she thought. If he doesn't know something, he admits it. At one point, he said that she is the bravest girl he has ever met. That made her heart flutter a little bit. Although, that comment may not mean that he is interested in her as a girl.

She went to another rally with Raphael and Guillaume the other day. It was really fun. Guillaume also told her that while Raphael and she are going to North Korea, Guillaume, André, Gaby, and Michelle will be going to South Korea. Guillaume said that if she and Raphael are detained in North Korea, they are going to contact the Canadian embassy in Seoul. Stephanie has also memorized the address of the Swedish embassy in Pyongyang, as there is no Canadian embassy there. Although they may have already been captured before reaching the Swedish consulate as tourists cannot go on their own without the guide. At least this is the best exfiltration plan that they could come up with in case they were detained.

Now they are on the way to Beijing. They will be landing in Beijing in less than an hour.

Stephanie looks at Raphael, who is sitting beside her. He is currently sleeping. Stephanie finds him very adorable when sleeping. In Toronto, he picked her up by Uber to go to the airport and they were stuck together for a fifteen-hour flight to Hong Kong, and then another three hours from Hong Kong to Beijing.

Raphael turns out to be a fun travel buddy. He is chatty and funny, too. He is a typical happy-go-lucky person. He often talks about his extreme adventures like alpine skiing, mountain climbing, and skydiving. Stephanie is super interested in skydiving. She has never done it but she is very eager to try. Stephanie's favorite adventures are water-based, like scuba diving, cliff jumping, and water rafting.

At some point during their flight, Raphael is also studying for his upcoming Royal College exam next year. He is reviewing the practice exams and notes. This is the serious side of him that Stephanie also likes. She finds that a guy who studies hard and works hard is very cool.

Once they land in Beijing, they pass through Chinese immigration and gather their luggage. Their next flight to Pyongyang is tomorrow, so they will stay overnight in Beijing. Also, today they will attend a briefing for their tour in a hotel near the train station. They will meet their fellow travelers and receive their North Korean tickets and visa there.

When passing the highway from the airport to the briefing hotel, Stephanie can see that Beijing seems to be more crowded than Toronto. Everything is very foreign here. The building architecture seems to be more advanced than in Toronto. The signs are mostly written in Chinese. Stephanie is used to living in Toronto where the city is multicultural. But here in China, she is a minority.

When they enter the conference room in the hotel, some travelers are already there. They introduce themselves. Some of them are from the UK, Netherlands, France, and Australia. And there is also another group, which is mostly of Asian descent. They are from China and Singapore. Only Raphael and Stephanie are from Canada.

A guy with dark hair and pale skin approaches Stephanie.

"Hi, what's your name?" he speaks with a British accent.

"I am Stephanie."

"I am Brad. Where are you from?" Brad asks.

"Canada. And are you from the UK?"

"Yes."

They chat a bit. She finds that Brad is pretty friendly. The reason he decided to visit North Korea is the same as her. It's because of curiosity. Back in Manchester, UK, he is a civil engineer. In the middle of her conversation with Brad, she cannot help but notice that Raphael is now surrounded by the Asian group. Some of them are attractive Asian girls. There are a few Asian men in the group but they are not as attractive as Raphael.

At two p.m., all the tour members have arrived and they start the briefing. Stephanie takes a seat in the front. Brad takes a seat on her left. Then, she notices that Raphael walks towards her and sits on her right. Although he seems to have just made friends with a group of people, he still sits beside her.

A man in his thirties walks towards the front and takes the microphone.

"Good morning, everyone. Thank you for coming to this very important briefing. My name is Matthieu. I was originally from France but I have been living here in Beijing for five years. I will be your guide for the next five days in North Korea. I speak English, French, and Mandarin," Matthieu says in English. It seems like he has done this briefing numerous times.

For the rest of the briefing, Matthieu tells them what they should and shouldn't do while they are in North Korea. He keeps telling them not to question North Koreans about their devotion to Kim Jong-un, the supreme leader, and his family. Keep being respectful towards their beliefs and culture. Also, they cannot wander around without a guide when they are there.

After that, he distributes their North Korean visas and tickets. Most of the people in the group will take an overnight train from Beijing to Pyongyang. Only four people will fly tomorrow, including her, Raphael, Brad, and another girl from China named Lindsay. Another guide, David, will also join them tomorrow.

After the briefing, Raphael and Stephanie check in to their hotel near the airport. Stephanie cannot sleep that night as she is too excited—and scared at the same time.

Chapter 5

Early December

Pyongyang, Day 1

Raphael looks at the view from his window seat at Air Koryo. It's the first time he gets a glimpse of the most mysterious country on Earth. From the plane's window, he can only see roads and farm fields covered with snow. But he knows that it's because the airport is quite far from the city center.

Unfortunately, Stephanie is not sitting beside him on this flight. She is sitting in a row behind him next to David, another guide who has just joined them this morning. Raphael is wondering how Stephanie feels right now. Is she as excited and nervous as he is? After all, this trip is her idea. And he got inspiration from her.

A few minutes later, their plane lands at Pyongyang Sunan International Airport at around three p.m.

Raphael feels super excited. He is in North Korea, a country he has never dreamt to visit.

The airport is small but it looks normal, except that the arrival terminal looks a bit deserted. Of course. North Koreans are not allowed to travel abroad without permissions from the government, and not many tourists are interested in visiting North Korea other than adrenaline junkies like Raphael and Stephanie.

At the immigration checkpoint, the officer checks his passport, visa, and entry card. The entry process is still similar to other countries. After that, Raphael waits for Stephanie, Brad, Lindsay, and David before getting to the baggage claim area.

After the baggage claim, they enter the custom area. This time the officers do a more thorough inspection of their luggage, passport, and electronic devices. Before the trip, Raphael was confident that he double-checked all the rules of what he should and should not bring. He also went over his phone as well to make sure that there is no forbidden material, like inappropriate photos, religious files, or publications about North Korea that he read a lot before this trip. Raphael also deleted all his search history related to North Korea in his phone. However, now he still feels nervous for some reasons.

The officer also carefully inspects his medical bag which mostly consists of over-the-counter medicines, first aid kit, and some vital signs kit. Luckily, they don't question him.

He finally can breathe again after he passes the customs. Lindsay is already there waiting while Stephanie, Brad, and David are still in the custom area. It's weird that he was cleared first even though Stephanie went to the custom before him. Are they more lenient towards Asians and more strict towards westerners? Raphael always makes sure Stephanie goes before him at every checkpoint. Although they haven't talked a lot since they met other travelers, they are still travel companions. Raphael instinctively always looks out for her.

Finally, Stephanie, Brad, and David appear. After that, they meet their local North Korean guide who has been waiting for them in the arrival hall.

The local guide, Nam Bok, seems decent and innocent. He speaks pretty good English with an accent. Raphael notices that Nam Bok doesn't refer to the country as North Korea but Democratic People's Republic of Korea (DPRK).

After that, it's the moment that Raphael has been fearing. This thing is only done in North Korea, and not in other countries.

They take away your passport.

During the briefing, he has been advised that their passport will be taken upon arrival. But when this really happens, Raphael feels vulnerable immediately. Whenever he travels abroad, his passport is his life. Now it feels weird that he doesn't have it with him. In his head, he quickly recites the full address of the Swedish embassy in Pyongyang, although it may mean nothing at this point. Even if he doesn't even know how to get there, at least it makes him feel better.

Raphael hopes that he made the right decision by coming here. Yes, he is looking for adventure. But he cannot deny that there are risks associated with this trip. He can't help but imagine the faces of people that he loves. His mom, dad, Gaby, Michelle, André, and Guillaume. What if he is detained here and he won't see them again?

Raphael glances at Stephanie to see her reaction when her passport is taken.

She doesn't show any hesitation. She just surrenders her passport to Nam Bok and continues talking to Brad.

Is Stephanie more enthusiastic when talking to Brad than talking to him? How come they get along so well? They haven't stopped talking since the briefing yesterday. Raphael starts to wonder if this trip is going to be as fun as he imagined. He sighs in disappointment and starts talking to Lindsay while they exit the airport.

@@@

DMZ, South Korea

André, Gaby, Guillaume, and Michelle are standing on the Korean border on the South Korean side in the demilitarized zone (DMZ). They arrived in Seoul yesterday night. And the first thing that they do in the morning is to visit the DMZ to catch a glimpse of North Korea, where Raphael is voluntarily trapped there without any means of communication.

They all stand there looking at the blue buildings, soldiers with guns, and the barbed wire fence.

The foursome is busy with their own thoughts but they are all thinking about the same thing.

Raphael and Stephanie.

Have they arrived there? Are they safe and can they go through without trouble?

Gaby squeezes André's hand very tightly. André senses her worry.

"Don't worry, Gabs. Raphael and Stephanie are very strong and very smart. I am sure they have prepared for the worst," André says to Gaby, and squeezes her hand back.

"I hope so. It's just scary because we cannot contact them," Gaby says.

"Thank God they will only be there for five days," Guillaume adds while putting his arm around Michelle's shoulder. Although Michelle doesn't seem as worried as Gaby, Guillaume knows Michelle is trying hard to hide it.

Michelle sighs and puts her arm on Guillaume's waist while leaning on his shoulder. "Yeah, I cannot imagine why people want to go there for five days. I wouldn't step in that country even for a second."

After being satisfied looking at North Korea from afar, they return to their rental car to drive back to Seoul.

Chapter 6

Pyongyang, Day 2

Stephanie is excited to explore Pyongyang with the group today.

Yesterday, they finally arrived in Pyongyang and went through the immigration easily. After that, they had dinner at one of the fancy restaurants at Ryomyong New Town, which was a new and modern area in Pyongyang. There were lots of high-rise condominiums here, as well as schools and commercial buildings. Stephanie was very surprised that there was an area like Ryomyong in Pyongyang. She imagined that Pyongyang was more old-fashioned.

At the dinner, the remaining members of the group who were taking the train to Pyongyang also arrived and joined them in the restaurant. By this time, she and Brad naturally always sat together, whether it was in the bus or in the restaurant, while Raphael always talked and sat with Lindsay. Stephanie was a bit disappointed, although she started to enjoy Brad's company.

What makes Stephanie and Brad really "click" together is their passion about music, especially classical violin. Brad used to take violin lessons until level six. Stephanie is a bit more advanced, as she finished her Associate Diploma level for her violin training. Brad is also fascinated about her profession as a music therapist. 'Unlike the other guy who is very skeptical about music therapy', she thought every time she glanced at Raphael.

When they checked in yesterday, ironically, she was rooming with Lindsay while Raphael was rooming with Brad. For some reason Lindsay got super enthusiastic. Maybe because she thought that she could switch rooms with Brad, and thus slept with Raphael and Stephanie wouldn't mind.

Of course that wouldn't happen. Although Brad was nice, Stephanie would not sleep in the same room with him.

Lindsay hasn't proposed anything, but last night she kept asking about Toronto, Canada, and finally a bit about Raphael. When did Stephanie meet Raphael? How did they meet? When Stephanie told Lindsay they only recently met, and she didn't know much about Raphael yet, Lindsay seemed to be a bit disappointed and then went to sleep not long after that.

Regardless, Stephanie reminds herself that the purpose of this trip is to experience North Korea. This is not a romantic vacation with anybody. She checks herself in the mirror one last time before coming out from her bedroom.

She goes down to the ground floor and enters the buffet room to have breakfast. The breakfast is held in a conference hall. She bets that this government-owned hotel must want to leave a good impression on the tourists.

Right away, she sees that Raphael and Lindsay are already there enjoying their breakfast like it's just the two of them. Raphael says something funny to Lindsay and she laughs a lot.

Stephanie tries not to look in their direction and starts walking towards the buffet instead.

The hotel serves some western breakfast food and some local Korean food. Stephanie serves herself two omelets, a piece of bread, and a bowl of seaweed soup.

She sees Brad is sitting with some other group members, so she joins them.

"Morning, Steph," Brad says.

"Hey, morning."

"So, what's your impression of this hotel?" Brad asks while eating his eggs.

"Umm. Better than expected, actually. It's kind of luxurious in my opinion. What do you think?" Stephanie asks. Stephanie is impressed with this hotel. It is a five-star hotel and very luxurious. The lobby is spacious and has a high ceiling. Even this buffet room can be a nice wedding venue. Although, she can feel that there is something inauthentic about this place.

There are a lot of propaganda paintings everywhere in the hotel including in their bedroom. It portrays Kim Il-Sung and Kim Jong-Il or some people in the rice fields looking very heroic. The paintings will have things written in Korean, like *Praise our Dear Leader and Eternal Leader, Long Live Our People, Blessed Joseon and Its Prosperity Forever.* She knows this because she can read Korean. The background of the paintings is usually red. These look like paintings from the nineties.

Also, just like everywhere in North Korea. It seems like everything is a set-up. But she doesn't want to voice it out loud here because it can be dangerous.

"Yeah. More luxurious than the majority of the hotels in Manchester," Brad says.

A guy from the Netherlands joins their conversation. He whispers to them, "Do you guys keep your underwear on when you shower?"

"What?"

"I heard they have cameras in every room, including in the bathroom," the Dutch guy continues. Now all of them are looking at him with horror and disbelief.

"Sssh, don't start to spread gossip. They can hear you," one of the Chinese girls whispers back to the Dutch guy.

An Australian guy from their group jumps in, "I think he is right. And I heard that there is one floor in this building that is dedicated for surveillance only. That's where they will watch your every single move, including in the bathroom."

Stephanie doesn't know if she believes them or not. But she makes a mental note that she will keep wearing her underwear when she showers.

@@@

Raphael cannot stop looking outside the window from the bus. Pyongyang is definitely more beautiful and more colorful than he imagined. There are a lot of squares, monuments, condominiums, and government buildings. The other thing that bothers him is the propaganda billboards everywhere. A lot of them portray the country's previous leaders, Kim Il-Sung and Kim Jong-Il, if he is not mistaken. He thought they were already dead. It's weird to see that they put the pictures of their deceased leaders everywhere. Also, these billboards have Korean characters written on them, which he doesn't understand at all. It bothers him.

There is not much traffic in Pyongyang like in Toronto. Here, he can see that most people are walking or biking. Maybe only certain people are allowed to have a car. Although there are not many cars, the capital city has a very wide road. He finds it weird. Again, maybe because the government wanted to give a good impression to tourists.

The people also seem to wear the same clothes. Either military uniform, all-black uniform, or white shirt and dress pants. It's weird to see that everybody seems very formal and reserved.

"Raphael, are you listening?" Lindsay calls him. It seems like she has just said something but he is too busy enjoying the view and not paying attention to her.

"Sorry, what did you say?"

"I say we should take a picture together."

"Now? But we haven't arrived anywhere yet. Hey, look, I notice that there is no traffic light! Instead, they put a woman in military uniform to manage the traffic. Don't you find it funny?" Raphael points out the street. Lindsay pouts.

Raphael doesn't understand why Lindsay seems to be more interested in him than in the scenery outside. He looks at other tour members. Especially Stephanie. Like him, Stephanie is looking out the window with great interest. Curiosity and excitement are all written on her face. Brad who is sitting beside her in the bus also shows great interest.

Once they get out of the bus, Raphael plans to run away from Lindsay as soon as possible. He would rather join Brad and

Stephanie as a third person rather than being tailed by Lindsay all the time. This morning when he entered the breakfast hall in the hotel, Lindsay was already there and asked him to sit with her at a table for just two people. Raphael had no other choice, although he preferred to join their group rather than exclusively sitting with Lindsay.

Finally, they arrive at their first stop: Mansudae Hill Grand Monument.

Raphael has seen these bronze statues of Kim Il-Sung and Kim Jong-Il on the Internet before coming to North Korea. Now he cannot believe that he is finally standing here in person. The statues are very gigantic. They have been warned that if they want to take a picture of the statues, it has to be the full statue. It cannot be the head only or half-body. As such, they cannot take selfies.

As predicted, Lindsay asks him to take a picture of her. And she keeps not being satisfied with the pictures. This reminds him of his sister, Michelle. However, Michelle is much more considerate than Lindsay. He has to retake Lindsay's picture probably ten times.

After Raphael finishes taking her pictures, Lindsay asks Stephanie who has just passed by to take a picture of her and Raphael. 'What, I haven't even taken a picture by myself?' Raphael is boiling inside, but he tries to stay calm.

Stephanie takes a picture of them politely. Raphael cannot help but notice that Stephanie looks really nice today. Although she is wearing a trench coat, black jeans and white shirt tucked in, it shows her strong body beneath the clothes that she wears. She also ties her hair into a ponytail, which he finds very cute.

Lindsay checks the pictures that Stephanie took, and as usual, she is not happy.

"Raphael, you didn't smile in the picture. You looked distracted," Lindsay says. "Stephanie, would you mind retaking?" Lindsay says to Stephanie.

"Of course," Stephanie says. But before she grabs Lindsay's phone, Raphael intercepts right away.

"That's okay, Steph, thanks. Lindsay, let's give her a break." Raphael forces a smile. Then he turns to Stephanie. "Let me help you take pictures, Steph," Raphael says.

Stephanie looks a bit surprised like she doesn't expect it. "Sure, okay. Thanks." She gives her phone to Raphael.

Raphael snaps several pictures. It is quite hard to get a good angle as he wants to focus on Stephanie but at the same time, he has to stand far to get the full statue. But luckily, he is pretty good at taking pictures thanks to having two sisters who always asked him to be their photographer. But when taking pictures of someone he likes, he doesn't mind at all. He even enjoys it.

He enjoys taking pictures of Stephanie.

It is clear that Stephanie is someone who doesn't take pictures often. She looks a bit shy. But that makes her even cuter. While Lindsay did a lot of extravagant poses like Instagram models, Stephanie just did a simple pose. Raphael likes it more.

"Please check, let me know if you prefer a different angle." Raphael gives the phone back to Stephanie. Stephanie looks at the pictures and says, "Wow, these are very good. Thank you, Raphael."

That's it.

She is not picky. She is not trying to be someone else she is not. She is not asking him to retake a thousand times like Lindsay.

"Do you want me to take a picture of you?" Stephanie offers.

"That would be nice. Thanks."

One more positive thing about Stephanie, she returns people's favors. Unlike Lindsay. Lindsay didn't even offer to help him take pictures.

Raphael really likes the pictures that Stephanie took. He really wants to send it to Gaby and Michelle to make them jealous. Unfortunately, there is no wi-fi nor data plan in North Korea. There is no way to communicate with the outside world. So, he has to wait until they leave North Korea, assuming they leave the country safely four days from now. Raphael shudders at his own thoughts.

Raphael realizes how much he misses Gaby and Michelle already, as well as André and Guillaume. He wishes that they were here with him. This trip reminds him of their trip last year to Singapore, Auckland, Geneva, and New York. He remembers the first time they met Guillaume; it was in Marina Bay Sands and Michelle asked Guillaume to take pictures of them. At that time, they didn't know that Guillaume was André's manager.

Raphael looks at Stephanie who is now taking pictures of Brad. He wants to feel a sense of familiarity again, especially in this foreign country where everything is... weird. And for some reasons, Stephanie's presence gives that sense of familiarity. Maybe because she is also from Toronto and she even has met his sisters and his best friends.

He walks towards Stephanie and Brad and sighs when Lindsay starts tailing him again.

Overall, Raphael really enjoys the tourist attractions that they have visited so far. After Mansudae, they stopped at Kim Il-Sung Square. Raphael was amazed by how big this square was. Matthieu, the tour guide, explained that this square was usually used for gathering, dances, and military parades. The view from this place was actually nice. The square was right beside the Taedong River. He could also see Juche Tower on the opposite side of the river. But their North Korean guide, Nam Bok, kept directing their attention to the Grand People's Study House building, which was a giant National Library Building located on the east side of Kim Il-Sung Square. There was a picture of Kim Il-Sung and Kim Jong-Il there. Nam Bok seemed to be very proud of this building. He kept telling them that this was one of the biggest libraries in the world, which had the most complete collections. Raphael had to resist himself not to laugh. He doubted that Nam Bok provided them with accurate information.

They also had a chance to ride the metro. Raphael didn't expect that Pyongyang had such beautiful metro stations, even better than some of Toronto's Subway stations. They stopped only at certain stops. He had a feeling that they were only shown the metro stations that were exceptionally nice and probably not all the stations were this nice.

After that, they stopped at the Arch of Triumph. Again, Nam Bok also seemed very proud of this monument. He explained that this monument was built to commemorate their liberation against Japan in 1945. He made it sound like it was North Korea who defeated Japan, while in reality, Japan lost the war because the US bombed Hiroshima and Nagasaki. Nam Bok also pointed out proudly that this Arch was taller than the *Arc de Triomphe* in Paris.

The next stop was the Korean War Museum. Here they displayed a lot of US military equipment that they managed to capture. One of the examples was the USS Pueblo that was captured in 1968. Nam Bok told them about several other North Korean victories against the US, which Raphael doubted really happened. During this visit, Raphael realized that he was actually in the enemy's territory. Although he was not a US citizen, he was aware that Canada had a good relationship with the US, which made Canada also an enemy of North Korea. He was glad when they finally left the museum.

Now finally they are in their last stop for the day, which is the Juche Tower.

Apparently, they have to pay extra if they want to go to the top of the tower. Raphael doesn't think twice to decide that he will go up. Stephanie also decides to go up, while Brad and Lindsay decide to stay. He is hoping that he can have one-on-one time with Stephanie. It has been very hard when Brad and Lindsay are around.

From the top of the tower, the view is incredible. It's sunset, so the sky is orange. The lights from the buildings have also started to illuminate the city. Despite being in probably one of the most dangerous destinations on Earth, it feels surprisingly peaceful from up here. When he looks down below, he is wondering what the North Koreans really think about their country, their leader, and their lives here. The government determines their fate. Whether they should live as farmers, factory workers, teachers, doctors, government officials, or military personnels. The closer the people are with the leader, the more likely they will become government officials or military personnel, and as such, they will be able to live in Pyongyang. To be able to live in the capital is such a privilege, per Matthieu earlier. Raphael feels extremely grateful that he wasn't born in North Korea.

Suddenly he remembers what Stephanie said when they were at André's place: *And when I return to the west, I may appreciate our freedom more. And I probably would not see Canada in the same way again after visiting North Korea.*

Now he understands what she meant.

Raphael searches for Stephanie. There she is. She is standing by the window, and like him, she is enjoying the sunset view of Pyongyang. Raphael walks towards her.

"Hey."

Stephanie turns to him and smiles. "Hey."

"You seem to be thinking. Can I know what's on your mind?" Raphael says.

"Sure. Hmm. I have always wanted to visit this place. I like that this tower is named Juche."

"What is Juche again? I know Matthieu explained it earlier. But I forgot." Raphael is never good at history.

"Juche is the main ideology of North Korea. It means self-reliant, economically, politically, and militarily. Although, if I were a country, I don't know if I would adopt this ideology. But as a person, I like it. You know, being self-reliant and independent," Stephanie explains.

Raphael already knows this about her. But the fact that she said it out loud to him, Raphael feels a new connection between them. So far, they only talked about their adventures. But they never really discussed deeper subjects like personal values like this.

"I know you are very self-reliant and independent, Steph. Also, you are very brave. However, sometimes it's also good to let other people take care of you," Raphael says.

Stephanie doesn't answer. She only looks at him with an unreadable expression.

"Anyway, thank you for giving me the idea of coming here. This is the adventure that I have been looking for," Raphael continues while putting his hand on her shoulder. Then, he gives her his most attractive smile that has melted a lot of girls' hearts.

After that he leaves her speechless.

Chapter 7

The next day, Stephanie is still thinking about what Raphael had said to her in Juche Tower. Although Raphael said it in a casual but thoughtful way, Stephanie knows that he was just flirting with her. Stephanie has so many guy friends and she has seen a few guys like Raphael. These guys know how to maintain their coolness around girls and then say one or two sentences that are very touching to the girls, and *voilà*, the girls feel great about themselves and cannot stop thinking about these guys that give them validation.

This morning during breakfast, Raphael sat with the group. Lindsay looked a bit sad. Raphael talked more to other people now, not just to Lindsay. As predicted, now more and more girls are charmed by Raphael.

Now they are visiting Kumsusan Palace of the Sun. This is where Kim Il-Sung and Kim Jong-Il were buried. To visit this place, they have been warned that they have to wear formal clothes, as this is considered a sacred place for North Koreans. As such, Stephanie is wearing her white shirt, black skirt, black blazer, and black tights. She glances at Raphael, who is wearing a suit without a tie. She has to acknowledge that he looks very handsome and very smart. No wonder almost all the girls in the group are falling for him.

Stephanie herself is spending more time with Brad; Conor, the Australian guy; and Peter, the Dutch guy. It feels very easy and natural among them. They are very chill as well, unlike Raphael who always makes her nervous.

After Kumsusan, they visit the Revolutionary Martyrs' Cemetery at Mount Taesong. A lot of generals and politicians were buried here. While enjoying looking at the cemeteries,

Stephanie is always looking out for Raphael. She tries not to do that but she cannot resist the temptation. Thus, she is always aware of where he is.

"Are you falling for him, too, like most of the girls here?" Brad, who is standing beside her, seems to notice her eye gaze towards Raphael.

Stephanie is panicking for a second. "I am not. Why do you ask?" she says quickly.

Brad laughs. "Relax. It's okay, Steph. Raphael is likable. No wonder he has a lot of fans."

"Why do you think he is likable?"

"I am rooming with him, remember? He is very pleasant and he told me a lot of funny stories. Also, he asked about you, too."

Stephanie's heart skips a beat, "Me? What did he ask?"

"He asked what we usually talk about. I said mostly about violin, classical music, and your profession as a music therapist. Then, he asked if I was into you," Brad says honestly.

"What? You must be kidding."

"I'm not." Brad is looking at her now. Stephanie doesn't know what to say. So, Brad continues, "Aren't you curious about what I told him after?"

Stephanie tries to relax. She never thinks that Brad is interested in her. But now she is curious.

"What is it, then?"

"I told him if I lived in Canada, I would be interested. Unfortunately, I live in the UK. And I am not someone who can do long distance." Brad throws her a smile. Stephanie feels flattered by his confession. For her, even if she and Brad were living in the same country, she hasn't been able to see herself falling for him. Yes, Brad is attractive. But she is only interested in him as a friend.

"Thanks for your honesty." Stephanie doesn't know what else to say. But she can feel that her face is getting red.

She glances at Raphael one more time. He is talking with two Chinese girls in their group. As if he can sense that Stephanie is looking at him, he turns towards her. It's too late to avoid his gaze now. So, she just smiles at him.

He smiles back at her.

That night, there is a banquet party. By now, everybody in the group starts to get to know each other and get comfortable with each other.

The restaurant serves them a lot of alcoholic drinks and some local Korean food like cold noodles, bibimbap, and Korean barbeque. This time there are also some local dance shows performed by local North Korean ladies in Hanbok. The atmosphere is like in a night club but with Korean folkloric music. Approaching midnight, people also start to get a bit tipsy and drunk. The North Korean ladies in Hanbok also join them for the drinks.

Stephanie enjoys the beer and the show. She limits her drink because she doesn't want to get drunk. Instead, she is enjoying the view of the capital city and Taedong River from the restaurant's window.

Suddenly, a voice from behind startles her.

"How is it going, Steph?" Raphael approaches her. He is carrying a drink in his hand.

"Great. What a fun night. I would never have imagined this kind of party in North Korea."

"Yeah, me, too." Raphael drinks from his glass.

"How about you? Do you enjoy our tour so far?" Stephanie asks. She noticed earlier that some of the North Korean ladies tried to engage in a conversation with Raphael. Wherever he goes, he always attracts ladies.

"Yes, I am. I don't realize that this is the vacation that I need. It feels like an escape." Raphael sighs.

"What are you escaping from?"

"From my reality. Work, my upcoming exam, it stresses me out sometimes." This is the first time Raphael opens up to her.

"Is being a doctor your own choice or your parents'?" Stephanie asks. She knows from her Asian friends that Asian parents have a lot of expectations on their children.

"My choice. Although my parents never explicitly put any expectation on me, I know that they work hard and they are successful. So, I want to follow their path. I don't want to let them down after all the privileges that they gave me. Moreover, I am the first child. So, I have to give a good example to my sisters."

"I see. I think you have already been a good example," Stephanie says.

"Thanks."

She can see that Raphael's cheek starts to flush. He may be drinking too much. Then he leans his head on her shoulder. Stephanie didn't expect this at all.

"I really want to listen to you playing the violin someday," Raphael suddenly says.

Stephanie chuckles. "Well, okay, someday. Are you into classical music?"

"Yeah, a bit. I started to love Chopin. How about you? Who is your favorite composer?"

"Uhh, that's a tough question. I have many. But particularly I like playing pieces with Allegro tempo."

"Allegro? What does that mean? Fast?"

"Yes, somewhere between one hundred to one hundred and sixty bpm. Music with allegro tempo usually evoke positive, joyful, and cheerful spirits."

"Just like you," Raphael says.

"So are you," Stephanie replies honestly. She decides to play along with Raphael. She likes the adventure that they are having now. Is Raphael doing this to other girls in their group? Is that why they are glued to him? Stephanie doesn't care. As long as she can guard her heart.

"Back to your question. One of my favorite composers is Dvorak. His music is very inspiring. Sometimes they are just simple and repetitive melodies but very deep."

"Again, just like you, Steph. You are down to earth, not complicated. But very deep." Raphael lifts his head from her shoulder and looks into her eyes deeply.

For one second, Stephanie thinks they are going to kiss, but then Matthieu announces that it's time to go back to their hotel.

Chapter 8

Pyongyang – Kaesong - Sariwon, Day 4

The next morning Raphael feels a slight headache. He was probably drinking too much yesterday. But he clearly remembers his conversation with Stephanie yesterday. Under the influence of alcohol, he just said whatever in his head without a filter. Usually, he complimented girls and flirted with them easily. But with Stephanie, for some reasons, he doesn't have the courage to approach her without alcohol.

Today they are going to drive to Kaesong City to stop at the border. The drive will take about two hours.

Inside the bus, Raphael sees that Stephanie is sitting alone. Brad is still behind talking with some other guys. Raphael doesn't waste his chance. After the progress he has made with Stephanie yesterday, he wants to sit beside her in the bus.

"Do you mind if I sit here?" Raphael asks Stephanie.

"Nope." Stephanie throws him a smile. She looks a bit tired too today. Everybody appears to still have a hangover after the party last night. Raphael notices that she is listening to music with her earphone. He is curious.

"What are you listening to?"

"Some sentimental violin music. Do you want to listen, too?" Stephanie asks.

"Sure."

Raphael has started to enjoy classical music after attending André's concert last year. Now he is excited to expand his classical music playlist. Apparently, Stephanie is listening to a piano and violin duet. The melody is very beautiful.

They don't talk much during the bus ride as they both are enjoying the sentimental music. On the way, Raphael notices that

Stephanie is falling asleep a few times. Her head keeps falling to the side. Raphael carefully places her head on his shoulder.

@@@

Stephanie finds herself falling asleep on Raphael's shoulder. When she wakes up, he is still asleep. Her earphone is still in his ear, so she takes it out carefully. She notices that he smells so good. Like an aftershave smell. Today he is wearing a navy-blue jacket, checkered shirt, and jeans like usual. He looks very cool.

She gently shakes his shoulder until he wakes up.

"Where are we?" Raphael finally wakes up and is a bit disoriented.

"We are at the border. Let's go."

Today they are visiting the Demilitarized Zone (DMZ) from the North Korean side. This is the place that she has imagined since she has learned about Korean history. She has visited the DMZ from the South Korean side multiple times. The fact that now she is standing on the North Korean side gives her the adrenaline rush.

Stephanie sees the Panmunjom flagpole which has the North Korean flag on the top. In the South Korea side in Daeseong-dong, there is also a similar flagpole that has the South Korean flag. The South Koreans put their flag first. Then, the North Korean put up their flag not long after to solidify their status. They also built a taller flagpole than South Korea's. Rumor has it that the North Koreans try to attract the South Koreans to defect to the North.

"Oh, now I remember. My sisters and my friends were here three days ago," Raphael says.

"Oh yeah, I remember Guillaume told us that they will be watching over us from the South. That's funny," Stephanie adds.

"I hope they are not too worried about us."

"They probably are. But you will meet them again soon. In what, three days?"

"That's true."

Stephanie wishes that she has someone who worries about her other than her parents. She thinks that Raphael is very lucky to have supportive friends and sisters. People say that we can judge a person by their close circle. Stephanie can tell that Raphael's close circle is made up of good people. So, Raphael must be a good person as well. Whoever girl Raphael ends up with will also be lucky to join his supportive friends and family.

After the DMZ, they head back north to Sariwon City, a folkloric village. The village transports them back to ancient times. There are historical buildings and houses. In the background, there is also Mount Kyongnam. The hike to the mountain only takes ten minutes. Raphael and Stephanie decide to hike without hesitation. They both are so used to rigorous exercise that this hike feels like an easy walk.

Once they arrive at the top, there is a pagoda that offers breathtaking views. They can see Sariwon City as well as the North Korean mountain ranges. Raphael and Stephanie enjoy the view in silence for a while.

When Stephanie walks to the right to capture the view from a different angle, she accidently trips and almost falls. But then a strong hand holds her waist to prevent her from falling.

"Are you okay, Steph?" Raphael's voice from behind her sounds alarmed. Stephanie is aware that her back is against Raphael. She turns towards Raphael and sucks a breath. They are standing very close to each other. Their bodies are now against each other. She can feel his lean body beneath his shirt. His hand is still on her waist.

"Yes, I am. Thanks." She feels her face start to turn red.

Raphael hasn't released his grip. They look at each other for a while. Then he lowers his gaze to her lips. For a second, she thought he was going to kiss her. But then he carefully releases his grip after she can stand steadily.

"Let's take a picture here. Both of us." He pulls out his phone.

@@@

On the way down from the top of the mountain, Raphael cannot ignore his accelerated heartbeat a while ago when he was holding Stephanie. What's wrong with him? For someone as fit as him, his heartbeat is usually below seventy bpm, even when he is standing or walking. But earlier, he was sure it was more than one hundred bpm, just like when he was exercising.

Is his feeling towards her getting stronger? He admits that he has been thinking about her these days. He tried to flirt with her sometimes, but it wasn't the same feeling as when he flirted with other girls. With other girls like Lindsay, he flirted just for fun and he flirted more obviously. But with Stephanie, he was a bit more careful. He doesn't want to scare her away. He doesn't want her to think that he is merely a flirty guy. Could she be the girl that he has been looking for?

Raphael secretly studies Stephanie who is walking beside him. She also appeared shy earlier. Raphael cannot forget the sensation while he was holding her firm and small waist. Her natural smell also drove him crazy. Her lips... Raphael quickly shakes his head.

Finally, they arrive at the village and they see their group is now playing soccer or dancing along with the locals in the field. Some local children are also singing and playing instruments. One of them holds a violin!

"Steph, look! That boy is playing the violin. Shall we come closer?" Raphael asks Stephanie. Her face also lightens up after seeing the boy with the violin.

"Sure. Let's go."

They approach the children and continue to listen to the singing and the violin. The songs that they sing sound like Korean folkloric songs. They sound very foreign to him, but the children appear very cheerful and lively. Raphael is wondering if they are forced to look happy in front of the tourists or they are truly happy. He can't tell.

Once they finish their songs, Raphael and Stephanie clap loudly for them. The children bow their heads shyly.

"Steph, you can speak Korean, right? Can you translate for me, please?"

"Sure."

Raphael approaches the boy with the violin.

"Hi, thanks for playing very beautifully. Can I borrow your violin for a second?" Raphael asks the boy. Stephanie translates what he says to the boy.

The boy nods and gives his violin to Raphael. Then Raphael gives the violin to Stephanie.

"Play for us, will you?"

Stephanie hesitates for a while. She is just looking at the violin. But after that she nods with determination and starts playing.

This is the first time Raphael hears Stephanie plays the violin. He is speechless for a while.

A strong and powerful melody comes out from the violin. Raphael has never heard this song before. It sounds foreign, patriotic, but beautiful and full of emotions.

Suddenly, everybody in the field stops doing what they are doing and their heads are drawn to the source of this melody.

Some people start to become emotional and drop to the ground and cry. What's happening? Raphael doesn't understand what's going on.

The song is under two minutes but the silence that continues after that lasts longer.

Why is nobody clapping for Stephanie? So, Raphael starts to clap.

The tourists that don't understand what's going on follow Raphael to clap.

Then Raphael sees Nam Bok, as well as their guides, David and Matthieu, walk towards them. They don't smile nor clap. Their faces look serious.

It seems like they are in trouble.

Chapter 9

"What were you thinking when you played that song, Stephanie?" Matthieu asks her when they are on the bus.

"Nothing. My intention was just to entertain the children by playing the song that they are already familiar with. Is it wrong to play the National Anthem of a country that we are visiting?" Stephanie asks.

Aegukka.

That was the song that she played earlier. It is the National Anthem of North Korea. South Korea also has the same name for the National Anthem, although with different lyrics and melody. But the song that she played was the North Korean anthem. That's why all the locals turned their heads to her and even got emotional.

"It will create a question. Like how did you know the song? Where did you learn it from? Now, I am pretty sure they are conducting thorough background research on you," David says.

Raphael jumps in. "If I were them, I would be so impressed. The fact that Stephanie played the National Anthem showed a great deal of respect towards this country. They should be grateful towards her."

"We never know what's in their mind," Matthieu says.

"Okay, what should she have played then? 'Twinkle Twinkle Little Star'? That's a song from the west! She would be captured immediately!" Raphael starts to get frustrated.

Nobody says anything.

After Stephanie finished the song earlier, Nam Bok recommended they leave the city right away. He hasn't said a single word towards them. But they all know that what happened in that field has already been reported to the government as tourists are closely watched here.

Raphael sighs and turns towards Stephanie.

"I am very sorry, Steph. I shouldn't have asked you to play."

"It's okay. I was the one who played willingly. Looking at how happy the children were, I just wanted to be part of it. I knew it was kind of dangerous what I did. When I played it, I felt an adrenaline rush. But I was curious what would happen. I guess I have to stop being an adrenaline junkie," Stephanie says.

Brad suddenly joins them. "Hey, Steph. It was impressive what you did. However, if something happened to you, in case you were detained, I will try my best to contact the Swedish embassy, the Canadian government, as well as the British government to rescue you."

"Thanks, Brad. Appreciated."

Now Stephanie realizes that she should not have risked herself like this. What a stupid act. It is not worth it at all. Now she has to bear the consequences. Would she be detained? Would she be sent to a concentration camp and do hard labor? How long will it take the Canadian Government to rescue her? Will they even rescue her?

For the first time in her life, she feels scared and alone. She imagines her parents' faces. She hopes that she will see them again.

Suddenly, Raphael covers her hand with his.

"Don't worry, Steph. I will be with you." His eyes are full of determination. She suddenly feels touched. She almost cries but she holds it. Instead, she just nods. Throughout the ride, her heartbeat accelerates due to anxiety and nervousness about what will happen to her.

Their bus finally arrives in front of the hotel. It is five p.m. in the evening. Tomorrow their flight back to Beijing is at nine a.m. What can happen in sixteen hours?

Unfortunately, it doesn't take sixteen hours to figure out. Once she hops off the bus, she sees two cars approaching. Once the cars stop in front of their bus, three military personnel come out from the cars and start talking to Nam Bok in Korean. Stephanie understands Korean very well, although they are speaking with a North Korean accent.

She freezes after hearing what they said. Her life is over.

The girl needs to come with us.

@@@

Raphael sees the fear in Stephanie's eyes.

"What did they say?" he asks her.

"They are going to take me," Stephanie says. Her voice is wavering but she tries to appear calm.

Raphael feels like his world falls apart. It's his fault. What's going to happen to her?

"Raphael, listen, once you return to Canada, could you please contact my parents? Also, will you try to contact the Ministry of Foreign Affairs? Although, I wouldn't expect that they will be able to rescue me," she says with a defeated tone.

Raphael grabs Stephanie's hand and walks quickly towards David, Matthieu, and Brad.

"David, Mathieu, Brad, they are going to take her away. Could you please try all means to contact the Swedish embassy as well as the Canadian embassy in Beijing?"

David and Matthieu look at them with fear. Finally, David nods. "Yes, we will try every possible means."

"Raphael, please. Can you promise to contact my parents? Tell them I love them," Stephanie begs. Raphael sees tears in her eyes.

"I am sorry, Steph. I cannot contact your parents. I'm coming with you," he says with determination. Stephanie's eyes widen.

"What? No…"

Before they can say anything, Nam Bok approaches them.

"Stephanie, unfortunately you have to come with them. It's okay. We don't know what they want yet. But it's better if you cooperate," Nam Bok says.

Stephanie takes a deep breath and nods.

"Okay." After that she releases Raphael's hand.

Raphael quickly grabs her hand back. "I'm coming with her, Nam Bok."

"They only requested her."

"I don't care. I'm not leaving her. I'm coming with her."

At this point Raphael knows that he is as good as committing suicide. But he doesn't care. It's his fault. She is his responsibility. He is full of adrenaline now. He cannot think straight. He cannot imagine leaving North Korea by himself tomorrow and leaving Stephanie behind.

Nam Bok sighs and then walks towards the military personnel who will escort them. They say something in Korean and the soldiers look at him carefully. One of them says something to Nam Bok.

"They ask who are you? What's your relationship with her?" Nam Bok asks him.

"I am her fiancé." Raphael blurts it out without thinking. He heard that when someone is punished in North Korea, the punishment will apply to three generations of the family. Raphael doesn't know if fiancé counts as family or not.

Nam Bok relays the message to the soldiers.

"You can come with us. But in a separate car," Nam Bok continues.

No way. Are they even going to see each other again?

Raphael doesn't waste any second.

"Stephanie, be strong. Be brave. At least you understand Korean. You will be able to survive, I have no doubt. You have done nothing wrong. You played the song with good intention. I am proud of you," Raphael says. He kisses the back of her hands. To make the scene more convincing, he kisses Stephanie on the lips and hugs her tight.

This is not the first kiss that he imagines with Stephanie. But he is surprised at how much strength that kiss gives him. He feels comfort. He feels like home. She kisses him back, full of emotions. He can sense her fear and vulnerability. At that instant he wants to protect her so badly.

Unfortunately, he has to release her.

"Thank you, Raphael. Be safe," Stephanie says, and then she follows one of the soldiers to the car. Nam Bok follows Stephanie into the car. At least she is not going to be alone. Although he doesn't know whether Nam Bok is on their side or not.

Raphael has no choice but to follow the other two soldiers to the other car.

Finally, they enter a building that seems to be a government building. The lobby has an impressive high ceiling, chandelier, and red carpet. There are also bifurcated stairs at the end of the lobby. Raphael feels like he is in Russia. This building gives him a "Kremlin" vibe.

But suddenly, they escort Stephanie to the corridor on the right and they escort him to the corridor on the left.

"I am coming with her!" Raphael starts to walk towards Stephanie. But one of the soldiers grabs his arm.

"You come this way," he says coldly.

"Hey, it's better not to resist at this point. Trust me," Nam Bok says to him.

Raphael looks at Stephanie on the other side of the corridor. The fear hasn't left her eyes but she nods at him with determination. Like she is saying, 'I will be okay. Go ahead and follow them.'

Raphael has no choice but to follow the soldiers.

They put him in a luxurious room that looks like an office. What building is this? Why does everything look very extravagant? Isn't North Korea supposed to be poor?

At the side of the room, there is a giant window covered by a red curtain. He starts to walk towards the window with a hope that he can figure out exactly where he is by looking out the window. He knows that he is somewhere downtown. He recites the address of the Swedish embassy in his head again. How far is it from here?

But before he can reach the window, Nam Bok stops him.

"Let's sit and talk first."

Raphael sighs and sits on one of the couches. One of the soldiers takes a seat in front of him. The other soldier, who is female, is standing by the door. The male soldier starts talking in Korean to him.

"Name?" Nam Bok translates it for him.

"Raphael Zhang."

"Date of birth and place of birth?"

"Toronto, June seventh." He also mentions his year of birth. He realizes that for a fit thirty-year-old male, he will most likely be sent to a labor camp. "Why don't you just check my passport? You have it, right?"

Nam Bok doesn't answer. The soldier continues with questions.

"Are you Chinese?"

"I am of Hong Kong descent." Raphael knows that North Korea has a good relationship with China. He hopes it is the same case with Hong Kong.

"Are your parents from Hong Kong?"

"Yes."

"What's your father's occupation?"

"Lawyer."

"What's your mother's occupation?"

"Teacher."

"What is your occupation?"

"Medical doctor." He hopes that his background as a medical professional can spare him from labor camp. Maybe he can work in their research facility. But then he remembered that North Korea often performs illegal medical experiments, like organ donations or performing a surgery without anesthesia. He quickly dismisses the thought.

"What's the purpose of your visit to North Korea?"

"For tourism. I want to accompany my fiancé." Raphael is wondering, if he was attached to a polygraph right now, would it detect any lie? However, he is good at lying. He lied all the time towards patients. He said to dying patients "You will be alright", even if they were on the brink of death. He told girls they were beautiful even though they were not.

After that, the male soldier says something to Nam Bok.

"We will be back shortly. Wait here," Nam Bok says to him, and then they both leave the room, leaving him with the female soldier.

Raphael cannot stop thinking about Stephanie. Is she holding up well there? Are they tougher on her because she is Caucasian? He hopes not.

It seems like he and Stephanie are not going to die soon. But everything that the North Koreans do here is very mysterious. He cannot really see where all of this is going. He turns to the female soldier. She looks very serious and cold. It's probably a good idea if he attempts to charm her so that he has a better chance not to be sent to a prison camp. However, at this point, his mind is on Stephanie. He cannot force himself to flirt with other women. He just doesn't have the capacity.

Half an hour later, Nam Bok and the male soldier enter the room. They bring him a set of clothes: black old-style top, black pants, and black shoes.

"Please change." Nam Bok puts the clothes on the table.

What is this? Why are they giving him formal clothes? Are they going to a trial now? Is this building perhaps a law court? But what would be the accusation? Does he have access to a lawyer?

"Where are we going?" Raphael asks Nam Bok. He cannot hide his fear now.

"You'll know later. Just change." Nam Bok seems to become more and more impatient towards him. Raphael notices that Nam Bok has also changed his clothes. Now he wears similar clothes as the ones he brought for Raphael.

"Okay, are you guys going to give me some privacy?" Raphael asks. Nam Bok and the soldiers are not moving nor saying anything.

"Fine," he snaps. He should have known that the word 'privacy' doesn't exist in North Korea.

He removes his shirt, his jeans, and his shoes, and resists the temptation to throw his clothes on the soldiers' face or Nam Bok's face. He looks at the pile of his clothes and realizes that his checkered shirt and jeans are very "American".

He reluctantly puts on the "North Korean" style of clothes. He is curious what he looks like now? A farmer? A fighter like Ip man? Or maybe just a plain North Korean worker.

"Put the pin as well," Nam Bok says.

Raphael looks at the red pin in disgust. It's a flag-shaped pin with Kim Il-Sung and Kim Jong-Il's faces. He has no choice. He puts the pin on his left chest.

"Okay, let's go," Nam Bok says.

"Where?" Raphael asks. As usual, they don't answer.

Raphael has no choice but to walk out with the soldiers and Nam Bok. He is just following them blindly without knowing where to go. The building is really big. They walk along several corridors for ten minutes. Raphael cannot remember how to get back to their room. He is wondering where Stephanie is right now. Will they reunite soon?

Finally, they enter a big room which looks like a small theater. There are several round tables where people who dress up like him sit. At the front there is a stage with an upright piano. It looks like there will be a musical show instead of an execution.

The male soldier points out an empty round table and motions him to sit there. Raphael complies. At least the soldier didn't ask him to stand on the stage to be tried or executed. He sighs with relief.

A few minutes later, the door beside the stage is opened and a few soldiers appear with a lady in Hanbok. They escort the lady to the stage and give her a violin. Raphael now realizes something after seeing the violin.

The lady in Hanbok is Stephanie.

Raphael's jaw drops open. He didn't recognize her at first because... she is extremely beautiful. They really transform her to become a noble-like lady. Her hair is styled as up-do and they put something like a chopstick to hold it together. Her Hanbok's colors are light pink and blue with a flower pattern. Although she is Caucasian, her beauty and her grace are comparable to an old-style noblewoman. Raphael remembers some historical Korean dramas that Gaby and Michelle used to watch. Stephanie is really similar to the strikingly beautiful concubines that usually appear in the dramas.

Stephanie's gaze suddenly turns to him.

The moment they look at each other, even though she is on the stage and he is sitting here, a warm and relieved feeling spreads throughout his body. He wishes he could hug her. But since he can't, he just smiles and nods encouragingly.

It seems like Stephanie is going to play the violin in front of these assemblymen! Raphael doesn't care about the positions of these people; he just feels very proud of her. So, they are not going to execute her, but she is going to play in front of them!

Stephanie smiles back at him. Raphael cannot imagine how she is feeling right now. Nervous? She doesn't show it. If Raphael had to play music in front of people, he would piss his pants right away.

The door once again opens. This time a bunch of soldiers are escorting a man in the middle. Suddenly everybody in the room stands and bows. Raphael has no choice but to stand and bow, too, although he doesn't know for whom he is standing and bowing. This man must be in a very high position that everybody must bow towards him.

Because Raphael is taller than most of the men here, he has a good view of the man who has just entered the room. He suddenly recognizes the man. *Holy.*

He is Kim Jong-Un.

Chapter 10

Pyongyang

At first, Raphael didn't believe his eyes. Is he really Kim Jong-Un? He has seen this guy in the news many times. This is one of the most feared men in the world. This is the guy who threatens the world with his nuclear missiles. And he does really look like him. And by the way the people in the room show great respect to this man, Raphael has no doubt that this man is really Kim Jong-Un.

Throughout his life, he has never imagined that he would see Kim Jong-Un in person. The aura in the room changes suddenly. He has goosebumps.

Then, a man dressed in black walks towards the stage and sits behind a piano. This man and Stephanie nod towards each other and they start playing their music.

Aegukka.

Now Raphael recognizes the melody. He is speechless. Again, Stephanie plays the National Anthem wholeheartedly and full of emotion. She does the vibrato that makes the music more alive and more touching. Listening to this music from Stephanie's violin gives a different vibe. Instead of the "communist" vibe, it becomes more like a nostalgic and patriotic vibe. Raphael is truly impressed.

When she finishes the National Anthem, the people in the room clap. However, the clap is very uniform and feels rehearsed. Only Raphael claps wholeheartedly.

Then, another man dressed in black walks towards the stage and whispers to Stephanie. Stephanie nods. After that the man says something in Korean to the audience. Raphael doesn't understand. So, he asks Nam Bok.

"What does he say?"

"The Supreme Leader allows her to play the music that she likes," Nam Bok whispers back.

Wow. The Supreme Leader must have really liked her performance.

Then, Stephanie starts playing again.

Raphael recognizes this music right away. He remembered listening to this music from Stephanie's playlist on her phone.

It's the first movement of Dvorak's four romantic pieces.

Cavatina.

The melody really touches Raphael's heart. It's simple and emotional. The tempo is allegro moderato. It's not very fast, and most of the time, it has a calming effect. Again, the vibrato from the violin really gives goosebumps. There are some sections that feel quite intense, like what they are experiencing right now. However, for a moment, Raphael forgot that he and Stephanie are in the hands of North Koreans. There is no guarantee of their safety. But for that moment, everything else matters less other than the music that she is playing...

She finishes the music gently and beautifully.

@@@

Back in the room, Stephanie cannot believe what has just happened for the past hour.

She played the violin in front of Kim Jong-Un.

Her brain still cannot process it. Is this really happening? Earlier she was so scared and confused. She thought they were going to interrogate her and then sent her to a prison camp. They did interrogate her about her background, but it was not like an interrogation for a criminal.

After that she was surprised when they dressed her in Hanbok. They said she was going to play Aegukka on the violin. She was not in the position to reject. They didn't mention that the

Supreme Leader would be there! At least they didn't send her to prison camp right away.

She cannot describe how relieved she was when she saw Raphael was in the room with her. Otherwise, she was going to play in front of these North Korean government officials who were very foreign to her by herself. When she played Dvorak's romantic pieces, her mind focused on Raphael. His presence made a huge difference. It made her so much calmer, although they both were in a dangerous situation.

After she finished playing, they escorted her out and put her back in her room. What will happen now? She doesn't know. She hopes that they are satisfied with her performance.

Not long after, the door in the room opens.

Raphael!

She is so relieved to see him. Seeing a familiar face in the middle of this very unfamiliar situation is a huge comfort.

Raphael quickly walks across the room and they both hug each other tight. She can feel his heart beating very fast.

"Steph, look at you. You played really well. I am very proud of you. Can you believe this? You played in front of..." He glances at the soldiers before continuing: "... the *Supreme Leader*," Raphael continues with a whisper.

"I cannot believe it either. Thanks for being here, Raphael. I couldn't imagine being there alone."

"You did great, Steph."

"I am not sure if it's over or not. They told me before I performed that I better give my best performance for my own good. What if they didn't like the music and they decided to punish us?" She is scared now.

"It's okay. We'll face it together. I cannot think of anyone who wouldn't like your performance. It was so perfect. So full of emotions," Raphael says.

"Thank you."

After that they sit nervously while waiting. Raphael is still holding her hand. Stephanie notices that he actually looks very cute in his North Korean outfit. But it is clearly obvious that he is not North Korean because he is taller and more muscular than other North Koreans.

Not long after, another soldier enters. They look at him nervously like they are waiting for a verdict.

"You both can go. Someone will drive you to your hotel," he says coldly.

Stephanie and Raphael hug each other again. She almost cannot believe her ears. They are free to go! She is very relieved until she can feel tears in her eyes.

She quickly changes her Hanbok to her street clothes with the help of a female soldier while Raphael is also changing in the other room. The soldier even tells her that she can keep the Hanbok and the violin! It's a complimentary gift. Wow.

Once they finish, they are escorted to the car. Inside the car, she feels extremely tired but very grateful. It was like she was given a second chance to live. She leans on Raphael and he puts his arm around her shoulder throughout the ride. He looks tired but happy as well. It's going to take them some time to process what has just happened. Their bodies are still full of adrenaline hormones.

When they arrive at the hotel, it's almost ten p.m. and all the guides and their tour group are welcoming them back in the lobby. They hug them tight and cannot stop asking questions about what happened. It's mostly Raphael who recounts their unique experience as Stephanie is too tired. Everybody is shocked and impressed to learn that they have just met the Supreme Leader.

"I don't want to lose sight of you again even for one second. Can we sleep in my room?" Raphael says once most of the crowd has left. Stephanie agrees. Brad also doesn't mind sleeping with Conor and Peter.

That night, Stephanie and Raphael fall asleep while holding each other. They become inseparable now after what they have been through together. Nobody else will understand how they feel. A new bond has formed between the two: a bond that is based on protecting each other, loyalty, as well as adventure.

Chapter 11

Pyongyang – Beijing

Early morning the next day, they pack their stuff, as they will catch a flight at nine a.m. Raphael is very relieved when Nam Bok finally returns his passport on the bus. At the immigration checkpoint, his heart starts to pound again. But luckily there is no hassle and they can pass through easily. He cannot wait to leave this country forever, and he will never come back.

But that's what he always told himself after he conquered very dangerous activities, like climbing mountains for example. He swore to himself that that was the last time he would ever climb a mountain that steep and dangerous. However, a few months later, he found himself climbing another mountain with similar difficulty or even more.

He needs to control his adrenaline addiction. The more adrenaline rush he has in his body, the more tolerance he develops.

Once they board the plane and take off, he sighs with relief. He looks at Stephanie who is sitting beside him. She appears tired.

"Are you okay, Steph?" Raphael asks.

"Yes, I am. How about you?"

"I am okay, too. Do you think you would ever come back to this place?"

"I would never say never but definitely not in the near future." Stephanie smiles weakly. "How about you?"

"Yeah, I had enough adventure in this place. It's a bit beyond my limit."

"Really? Ha ha. At least we now have seen the country ourselves. Otherwise, we will be curious forever."

"That's true. Although, we would never know the real North Korea. Every place that we visited there has probably been staged."

"That's true. Well, at least we have seen the real Supreme Leader. I hope he was real. Not a body double."

"Ha ha. I hope so, too. But we would never know."

Once he lands in Beijing and turns on his phone, he receives dozens of texts. From his mom, dad, Gaby, Michelle, André, Guillaume, and some of his colleagues from work. He is relieved that he can contact his family and friends again.

After retrieving their luggage and saying goodbye to Brad, Lindsay, and David, Raphael and Stephanie go up to the departure terminal again to catch their next flight back to Toronto. They have six hours to kill.

Before reading all his unread messages, he sends a mass text to everybody informing them that he has arrived in Beijing safely. Stephanie does the same. After that Raphael scrolls over his phone to reply to all the unread messages.

A message from André gains his attention:

Hey Raphael, I hope you are still alive. We made a last-minute decision to stop by in Dubai for a few days. We have booked a one-way ticket from Beijing to Dubai for you and Stephanie as well. Please find your flight schedule and reservation number in the below screenshot. Don't worry about the flight and accommodation costs. It's a gift for you for staying alive. I hope you can join us in Dubai. André.

What? Is André kidding? Raphael cannot believe what he has just read. He checks the reservation number on the airline website and finds his name on a flight that will depart three hours from now.

He glances at Stephanie who is sitting beside him. She is also going over her unread messages for the past five days.

"Steph, umm...instead of going back to Toronto, do you want to join my sisters and my friends in Dubai?" Raphael asks her carefully. He thinks it would be fun if Stephanie can join them in Dubai. After all the stressful experiences in North Korea, maybe they should continue with a proper relaxing vacation.

"What? Dubai? Are they there now?"

"Yes. They have booked two tickets for us. Here, look." Raphael shows his phone to Stephanie. Yeah, why not? He will not start working until January anyway. He hopes Stephanie also has some time off.

Stephanie looks like she is thinking hard. Raphael crosses his fingers.

Finally, Stephanie turns towards him and smiles.

"Yeah, why not?"

@@@

Beijing – Dubai

Stephanie cannot believe that she has just said yes to join Raphael's sisters and friends in Dubai. She definitely likes spontaneous trips, but she usually does it alone. She feels nervous. Could this trip be a turning point between her new friendship (or relationship) with Raphael? She doesn't know how to define their relationship right now. She definitely feels something for him. She feels safe and secure around him. But what about him? The fact that he accompanied her all the time when she was taken in North Korea, was that telling her that he cared about her as more than just a friend? Or was it just because he felt responsible as they traveled together? It's hard to tell because he is always casual and flirty around women.

She looks at Raphael who is sitting beside her from the corner of her eyes. They are now inside the plane on the way to Dubai. Raphael is reading his exam materials again. Now that the danger has passed, their adrenaline hormones have slowed down and they are not in a fight or flight mode anymore. As such, they don't need to hold onto each other again like yesterday. But if there is romance between them, regardless of whether they are in danger or not, they would hold onto each other, right? Stephanie doesn't know what to think.

Why would his friends invite her? She only met Gaby, Michelle, and André once. And Guillaume twice. She is not sure what to expect. From what she knows, if a man invites you to spend time with his friends, it means something. However, in her case, it's Raphael's friends who always invited her, not Raphael himself. Maybe it's his friends who want him to be in a relationship but not Raphael himself. Stephanie is a bit disappointed.

Behind her strong appearance, of course deep down she is still a woman. Although she enjoys being single, she is still longing to feel connected, to be understood, and to be protected. At the same time, she wants to love someone, too.

Chapter 12

Dubai, Day 1

They finally land at Dubai International Airport. After retrieving their luggage, Raphael checks his phone. André hasn't texted him again. He doesn't know at which hotel they will be staying.

Apparently, when they exit the gate, familiar faces have been waiting for them in the arrival hall.

"Raphael!" Michelle shouts excitedly. Gaby, André, and Guillaume are also there.

Without thinking Raphael runs as fast as he can with his luggage towards them. To be able to see his family and friends in person again is such a blessing. He really feels tears in his eyes.

He hugs Gaby and Michelle all at once. They hug him back very tight. It feels so good to be with his family again and to be free from the North Korean regime.

"Raphael... I... really... hate... you," Gaby says while hitting his shoulder for every word she said. Tears are falling from her eyes too. "Why do you keep endangering yourself like this? Don't you realize how scared I was?" Gaby continues.

"I know, I know. I'm sorry. I won't do it again. I promise. I was just too curious. Too excited." He tries not to cry during this emotional moment.

Michelle steps in. "Yeah? Really? Promise with what? You always said that you will stop your crazy adventures but you keep doing them." Michelle doesn't cry but her face is red. Although Michelle seems angry, Raphael knows that she is angry because she loves him and she is too scared to lose him.

"Well, what can I do?" Raphael sighs.

"I'm sorry, everyone. I should not have given him the idea of going to North Korea," Stephanie says while releasing herself from Guillaume, who just gave her a hug.

"It's not your fault, Stephanie. My brother is always crazy for extreme adventures. If it's not North Korea, it's probably something else more dangerous," Michelle says.

"It's so good to see you again, Raphael." André gives him a hug, and so does Guillaume.

"Hey Raphael, did you lose weight? They didn't feed you well in North Korea?" Guillaume asks while glancing at his body.

"Stop, Guillaume. I was only there for five days. I didn't lose weight." Raphael pouts. Did he really lose weight? He hates it when people mention it. Maybe this is because of the stress for the past forty-eight hours.

André jumps in, "Don't worry Raphael, he is just teasing you because he is missing his gym buddy. You look great, man. Let's get out of here and tell us everything that happened there."

@@@

They sit on the patio in one of the restaurants in Dubai Marina near Palm Jumeirah. From where they sit, they are surrounded by Dubai's tall skylines, yachts, and water views. Their hotel is also nearby. It's a three-bedroom suite, each with an en-suite bathroom, in one of the nice resorts in Palm Jumeirah. Earlier, Raphael and Stephanie left their luggage to the hotel's bellboy.

Dubai feels very different from Pyongyang. Now, everything is written in Arabic and English, while in North Korea, everything is written in Korean. Here everybody has freedom to speak, to go anywhere they want, and to laugh. The weather is pleasant that afternoon. Not too hot and not too cold. It's a perfect time to tell the group about their adventure in North Korea. André, Guillaume, Gaby, and Michelle have bombarded them with questions about North Korea. Stephanie lets Raphael take the spotlight and recount their experience.

"And by the time we went down from that mountain... what is it called, Steph?" Raphael tries to remember.

"Mount Kyongnam," Stephanie says.

"Yeah, there you go. Anyway, after that, this was when it started to get thrilling. I saw a group of children playing music. One of them was holding a violin. So, I borrowed the violin from him and asked Stephanie to play. I know Stephanie plays classical violin. You know how passionate I am about classical music..."

"Are you really?" Gaby cannot suppress her grin. André, Guillaume, and Michelle say nothing and only smile to themselves.

"Yes, I am. And after that, Stephanie played this foreign but beautiful melody. It sounded very patriotic and touching. In the beginning, I didn't realize what music that was. It definitely didn't sound like western music. And suddenly, everybody in the field was speechless. Some people started to become emotional, some were crying, some were fainting..."

"Nobody fainted, Raphael." Stephanie jumps in.

"Oh, maybe I remember it wrong, then. Anyway, can you guess what song Stephanie played?" Raphael throws a question for everybody to guess.

"'The Star-Spangled Banner'?" Guillaume answers with the USA national anthem.

"Don't be silly. If Steph did that, she wouldn't sit with us right now. She would have been executed on the spot. Steph played the national anthem of North Korea. What is it called, Steph?"

"Aegukka."

Then Raphael continued recounting what happened after. They were taken to an impressive government building, they were asked to change into a Korean outfit, and then Stephanie played the violin for Kim Jong-Un.

André, Guillaume, Gaby, and Michelle all look at them in disbelief.

"Kim Jong-Un???" Guillaume looks at them in a mixture of horror and impression.

"Are you joking??" Gaby's jaw drops.

"You mean you saw him in person?" Michelle looks very shocked.

Now looking back, Stephanie can laugh about what happened. These new friends keep saying that they are impressed that she got called to play the violin in front of the Supreme Leader himself. That means her violin skills must be exceptional. Throughout her life, she is used to giving herself validation. Now that someone else gives it to her, she feels good. She also feels accepted in this new circle of friends.

But more importantly, she likes the way Raphael talks highly of her in front of his sisters and his friends. Although it was Stephanie who played the violin, Raphael is the one who is beaming with pride.

She and Raphael also inquire with the group about their trip to South Korea.

Gaby is enthusiastic about her trip. "Well, it wasn't as intense as your trip to the North obviously. But we definitely had a lot of fun. We went to see the DMZ the next day after we arrived in Seoul, to catch a glimpse of the country that you guys were stuck at, then we visited Gyeongbokgung Palace, Namsan Tower, Gangnam Street, and we did some shopping."

"That sounds really fun. Did you meet any Korean actors or boy bands?" Stephanie asks.

"Oh, yes! Guess who we saw from afar? Hyun Bin!" Michelle cries enthusiastically. "It looked like he was in the middle of shooting a new movie or drama. I was about to ask for a photograph but Guillaume didn't allow me. So, I only took pictures from afar."

"No way! You are so lucky! I don't know which one is better. Meeting Kim Jong-Un or Hyun Bin." Stephanie can feel the excitement from Gaby and Michelle as well.

"Which one is Hyun Bin, again? Is he really that handsome? More handsome than me?" Raphael asks with a frown.

"Hmm...handsome is relative." Gaby tries to be diplomatic.

"Okay, enough about Korean guys. What are we going to do for the next few days?" Guillaume switches topics.

"How about skydiving?" Raphael proposes.

"Oh, c'mon, Raphael. Not again." Michelle rolls her eyes.

"Michelle, do you know that statistically speaking, skydiving is safer than driving a car?" Raphael replies.

"I think I will pass for skydiving. It's too much for me," André says.

"Me too. I still want to live. Sorry, Raphael," Gaby says.

"I prefer to go shopping," Michelle says.

"I prefer to accompany Michelle shopping," Guillaume says.

Raphael is looking at them with disappointment. Then, he turns his head towards Stephanie.

"Steph? How about you?"

Stephanie doesn't need to think twice. She has wanted to try skydiving for such a long time.

"I am in." She cannot hide her smile.

@@@

That night in the three-bedroom suite, Raphael and Stephanie end up sharing a room again. At least there are two queen-sized beds. Gaby asked him earlier if this sleeping arrangement was okay for him and for Stephanie who haven't known each other that long. Raphael doesn't complain. In fact, he enjoys it. He is relieved when Stephanie agrees to share a room with him, too.

Now he is inside the room trying to book a spot for skydiving while Stephanie is showering in the bathroom. Raphael tries not to imagine Stephanie in the shower, but it's hard. He is a man after all.

After that, Stephanie comes out from the bathroom. As much as he hopes that Stephanie is only wrapped in a towel and nothing else, she comes out already in her pajamas, even though her hair is still wet and wrapped in a towel. Raphael still finds it very sexy.

"Hey, Steph, the earliest spot available for skydiving is this Thursday at two p.m. Are you okay with this?" Raphael asks.

"Yes. That's perfect," Stephanie answers.

"Great. I will book it then."

After that, it's his turn to shower. He takes a warm bath and shaves. He feels good and clean afterward. Then he realizes that he forgot to bring clean clothes to the bathroom. Damn. He cannot walk out from the bathroom naked because it will scare Stephanie off.

He looks around and is relieved when he finds a bathrobe hanging behind the door. He wears the bathrobe and walks out from the bathroom. He finds Stephanie standing by the window admiring the view from their fifth floor suite. He can hear the wave sounds, and the views of the night ocean and the Dubai skylines illuminated with night lights are stunning.

"How are you doing, Steph?" Raphael stands beside Stephanie to admire the view together.

"I'm doing great! I'm tired but excited. This is my first time in Dubai. I'm happy that your friends and sisters invited me here." Stephanie smiles.

"Me, too. This is also my first time in Dubai and I'm glad that you can join us here."

They enjoy the view in silence for a while.

"I'm also glad that I finally found someone who is also adventurous. Are you always like this, Steph?" Raphael asks.

"Yes. I always like adventure because it makes me more confident. It also makes me feel good about myself. Like doing something that I initially thought I wouldn't be able to do, but then I did it. I feel accomplished. How about you? Are you always this adventurous?"

"When I was a kid, no. I was a nerdy kid. In the beginning, I started doing these things just to prove to others that I could do it.

You know, being an Asian man who was born and grew up in a western world has its own challenges. So, I started playing hockey and doing more sports to appear more macho. But then, I ended up liking them. I find that my love for sports and adventure goes hand-in-hand with my love for studying. It even enhanced it. I become more open to experience and more curious to learn things."

"I can relate. Your love for sports and adventure is like my love for violin and classical music. I used to be very shy and feel out of place because I'm a tomboy and I don't enjoy girly stuff like other girls do. I have more guy friends than female friends. That's why sports and adventure feel natural to me. At one point, to feel more like a 'girl', I picked up the violin. It turns out that I really love it. I love the sound it produces and the emotion I can convey through my violin."

"I can see that. It's good that you finally find something to counterbalance you as a person but without changing yourself."

"That's true. Like I don't stop doing sports and you don't stop studying. But we find something that is more 'normal' for our circumstances, I guess."

"But honestly, Steph, even if you don't play violin at all, I am sure there are guys that find you attractive because of your sporty and adventurous nature," Raphael adds. *Like myself.*

Stephanie chuckles, "Ha ha. Most of them see me only as a friend or a gym buddy. I don't think they find me attractive *that way.*"

"I find you attractive the way you are." He looks deeply into her eyes when he says that.

Stephanie is speechless for a second. Raphael resists the temptation to kiss her on the lips.

"Raphael, stop flirting with me. What if I fall for it?"

"Then, so be it. And I am not flirting at this moment. I am telling you the truth," Raphael says. Before Stephanie can say anything else, he puts both his hands on her shoulders and turns her body to face him. Then he gives her a light kiss on the forehead.

"Let's go to sleep. We will have a long day tomorrow," Raphael says.

Chapter 13

Dubai, Day 2

Stephanie's excitement for Dubai starts to wear off on the second day.

Today, they explore Burj Khalifa, the tallest building in Dubai, and maybe in the world. They admire the view of Dubai from the one hundred and forty-eighth floor, where they can see other skyscrapers, highways, the Persian Gulf, and the desert. However, she realizes that everything in Dubai looks very luxurious. She is embarrassed to admit that she prefers Juche Tower in Pyongyang rather than Burj Khalifa. She prefers to enjoy a city that conveys more history than just luxury. Even the hotel that they sleep in feels like too much.

By now, she figures that this is the lifestyle that Raphael's friends live in. She remembers André's suite in Shangri-La in Toronto. And now the luxurious vacation that they booked. Who are these people, really? On a day-to-day basis, André and Guillaume are always extremely well-dressed. Their outfits are simple but very elegant. They look like models for luxurious menswear brands. Gaby and Michelle also dress up very nicely. Nowadays, many women dress up in revealing clothes. But Gaby and Michelle's dresses accentuate their petite and feminine figures in a classy but modest way.

Only Stephanie and Raphael dress up casually.

At least Raphael wears something casual, a checkered shirt and khaki shorts. While Stephanie only wears a boring blouse and jeans. She is not prepared to prolong their vacations to Dubai. Her original plan was only to visit North Korea and then return to Toronto.

After Burj Khalifa, they visit Dubai Mall. Again, it's another gigantic and luxurious mall that has everything inside, including a waterfall, aquarium, VR park, cinema, and even a haunted house!

Inside the mall, Michelle and Guillaume decide to go shopping, while André and Gaby decide to check out a bookstore. This leaves Stephanie and Raphael alone, just the two of them. Stephanie feels like finally she can breathe.

"Are you okay, Steph?" Raphael checks in. They decide to exit the mall and just enjoy the water view from the promenade right outside the mall.

"Yes. It's just that I'm not used to all these extravagant and luxurious things. I feel out of place. I prefer visiting old cities or being in nature."

"Oh, I feel the same. This is too much for me, too."

"Really? I thought this was your lifestyle."

"Nah. This is more André and Guillaume's lifestyle. But not mine. I am only an ER resident, remember?"

"What do André and Guillaume do for a living?"

"André owns a private equity firm and Guillaume has his own artist management company."

"And how did you meet them? They are from Quebec and not from Ontario, aren't they?"

"Yes. Long story short, Gaby, Michelle, and I met them last year in Singapore during our vacation. André and Guillaume were there for work. But after that André fell in love with Gaby and Guillaume fell in love with Michelle. When we returned to Canada, André and Guillaume moved from Montreal to Toronto to be closer to Gaby and Michelle."

"Nice."

"I know what you are thinking. I have known André and Guillaume for quite some time and they are good people and not snobby at all. Otherwise, I wouldn't let my sisters date them. Their lifestyle can appear extravagant but that's because that's how they grew up, I think. You have played squash with Guillaume a couple of times, and he is very approachable and he really likes you. I bet he cannot wait to make you one of his gym buddies.”

“Ha ha, that would be fun. What about André? Is he always this quiet?”

“Oh, yes, he is very introverted. It took quite some time for Michelle and I to get to know him, too, in the beginning. But now that we do, he is a very loyal friend and he is the wisest among us although he is younger than Guillaume and I.”

“How about your sisters, Gaby and Michelle?” Stephanie now becomes curious to get to know Raphael’s close circle. She also enjoys listening to how Raphael talks highly about them. This is also what she likes about Raphael. He seems to always see the best in other people.

“Gaby is very sweet and sensitive. She and André are very similar. They are very thoughtful and caring. Michelle can be blunt sometimes, err... like me, but she never has bad intentions. She is funny and chatty. But wait until you watch her perform ballet on stage, you will be impressed. She is very elegant but strong.”

“I can see that.”

“What about yourself? Do you have any siblings?”

“No. I’m an only child. I always wonder how it feels to have siblings. Looking at you and your circles, now I can see how fun it is.”

“I see. André and Guillaume are also the only child. But look at all of us now. We are like brothers and sisters. You are part of us now, Steph,” Raphael says genuinely.

Stephanie is touched by what Raphael has said. Although they are still exploring their feelings towards each other, Raphael doesn’t hesitate to include her in his circle. She is aware that with Raphael’s cultural background, family and friends are very close. In his culture, being in a relationship with a person also means being in a relationship with the whole family. This is something that she also values in life although her culture is more individualistic than family-oriented.

From what Raphael has explained, she also feels relieved that Raphael's circle is not as snobby as she thought based on this luxurious vacation. She starts to feel less out of place.

However, right after she feels more relaxed, she feels a familiar warm discharge coming out from her pelvic area.

Damn. She forgot that it's the time for her period to start. She is panicking. She didn't pack any feminine products as she initially thought she would have been in Toronto by now.

Raphael seems to sense her uneasiness.

"Steph? What's going on? Is everything okay?" He puts his hand on her shoulder and turns her body to face him.

Oh no. Why does this have to happen when she is with Raphael? What could be more embarrassing than this? She takes a deep breath, tries to regain her composure. They both are adults. It's nothing to be embarrassed about, right? She tries to convince herself.

"I have to go to the pharmacy." She looks at the floor when she says it and starts walking towards the mall.

"Wait. Is it your period?" Raphael grabs her arm. She nods.

"Go to that washroom and wait there. What do you usually use? Tampons, pads, menstrual cups, or period underwear?" Raphael sounds all-business and is not awkward at all.

"Tampons."

"Okay. I will bring it soon."

"Thanks." She feels so relieved that she doesn't have to go around the mall herself to find a pharmacy. After that Raphael releases her arm and walks towards the opposite direction while Stephanie walks towards the bathroom.

While waiting inside the bathroom booth, Stephanie cannot stop thinking how gentlemanly Raphael is. He is always ready to help in an emergency situation. She finds that being reliable is a very attractive trait.

After that, a lady calls her name and slides a pack of tampons from below the door. She mutters thanks and feels relieved to have what she needs.

@@@

By the time they arrive at their hotel, Raphael feels tired but satisfied. He liked spending time with Stephanie today. They became more and more comfortable opening up towards each other. She looked a bit embarrassed after he solved her period issue today, but he found it cute. He told her that with two sisters and his job as a doctor, women's periods are not a big deal.

But he lied.

He realizes that Stephanie is a woman after all. Sometimes, he feels very comfortable with her to the point that he forgot that she is a woman, not one of his guy friends. But he does feel a strong attraction towards her regardless of her tomboy-ness. Now he has a hard time getting rid of his thoughts about Stephanie's woman-ness. Like her sweet and pleasant scent, thick brunette hair, and pale but smooth skin. Her face is also pretty and she has a youthful look. She looks like she is in her early twenties instead of 28 years old. He even thinks that her flat chest, flat bum, and muscular body are unique. He estimates her height is about one hundred and seventy centimeters. At least he is still eight centimeters taller than her. More importantly, she is different from most women he encountered.

Raphael walks towards the kitchen to grab a drink. Their suites feel emptier as the girls are currently having a relaxing night in the pool. André is probably working somewhere and Guillaume is probably in the gym working out.

On the way to the kitchen, he passes the living room and he finds André sitting there, busy working on his laptop.

"Is Guillaume in the gym?" Raphael asks while filling his glass with a cocktail from the fridge in the kitchen.

"Yes, I think so. Where else?" André replies.

"You are not joining him?" Raphael takes a seat beside André.

"Nah. I have some work to do."

Stephanie is right. André seems more withdrawn and quieter than usual since their arrival yesterday. He didn't say much when they had lunch at the Marina yesterday and also today at Dubai mall. Is he sick? Raphael is worried as usual.

"Is everything okay, André?" Raphael drinks his cocktail and tries to act like this is just a casual chat. André seems a bit hesitant before closing his laptop.

"Yes. Everything is okay. I just have a slight chest pain, but it's nothing serious."

Raphael becomes alert right away. "Hang on. Chest pain? Since when?"

"For the past few months maybe. But it has nothing to do with the surgery or my heart condition. All my test results including ECG, echo, stress test, and MRI, look good."

"And when was the last time you did these tests?"

"A few weeks ago. Before this trip. I have told my doctor about the chest pain. After reviewing all the test results, he concluded that it is more psychological than physical."

"Like because of anxiety or stress?"

"Yes."

"Do you wanna talk about it?"

Again, André seems hesitant. Usually, André is pretty open discussing his physical health with Raphael. But they never really talk about his mental health.

"Part of it is because of work. There are so many things to do and so many things I don't understand. Maybe I put too much pressure on myself because this is my dad's legacy, you know. But this is still manageable," André explains.

"Okay. So, you are stressed partially because of work. And what would be the other part?"

André sighs before answering. "When I think about my future with Gaby."

Raphael is shocked hearing this answer. Maybe he should not have asked André in the first place. He regrets it now. No matter how close he is with André, if André ever hurts Gaby, he will not let it slide.

"What do you mean?" Raphael tries not to get carried away.

"Don't worry. I am still very much in love with Gaby. Even stronger the more I spend my life with her. She is the one for me. I knew it from the beginning. But that's what worries me. I doubt myself all the time. Am I strong enough to be her husband? Am I strong enough to be the father of our children? What if I have to do another surgery in the future? What if my heart suddenly stops again? She has been through a lot when taking care of me after my surgery. I don't want her to go through that again."

"Okay, let's assume the worst. Let's assume that you are as weak as you have just described. What are you going to do? Break off your engagement? Ask her to find a healthier guy?"

"No, I wouldn't do that. But I will let her decide what's best for her and I will always respect her decision."

"I know she will not leave you."

"Yes, she is too selfless."

"That being said, let's focus on what you can do to make the situation better for everybody. Or are you going to do nothing and let this anxiety and stress take control of your life? Don't make me start a lecture on the impact of stress on cardiovascular health."

"So, what should I do, Doc? I am not good at stress management." At least André seems to relax a bit after talking out his problem. Their conversation becomes lighter now.

"Let's see. Do you exercise regularly these days? It can help with stress. What exercise did your doctor recommend?"

"I did some light exercises like sit-ups and push-ups. Although it's mainly for the sake of appearance..." André pats his perfect abdomen over his shirt. "...more than my health. Appearing strong in front of Gaby is the least I can do."

Nobody would ever guess that someone as young and as fit as André could suffer from heart disease. Although André is half-Asian and half-Caucasian, his body type is more Caucasian, meaning that he can build muscle easier than other Asians, unlike Raphael, who has to spend time in the gym twice longer than his Caucasian friends to achieve the same result. He imagined Guillaume is currently sweating in the gym while he is sitting here drinking cocktails. He swears to himself that he will hit the gym tomorrow.

"Also, my doctor said running, cycling, and swimming are good for me as long as I don't overexert myself," André continues.

"Oh, yeah, Gaby told me that you like swimming."

"Yeah, but I don't want people to see my surgery scar. I know it's trivial. But it really affects my self-esteem to some extent."

"C'mon, André. People will notice your six-pack more than your scar."

"Nah, they will notice my scar and forget to admire my six-pack."

"And why does it matter? Gaby still finds your physical appearance attractive, right? Isn't her opinion what truly matters?"

"That's true. But I hate it when people look at my scar with pity."

"I think you will get used to it and be less self-conscious over time. And how about playing piano to relieve stress?" Raphael continues.

"I don't know. Honestly, I don't find playing piano as enjoyable as before. I enjoy listening to Gaby's playing. It makes me less stressed. But aside from that, I don't find my reason to play piano anymore except for when Gaby asks me. But I think she noticed that I only played to make her happy and so she stopped asking these days."

'Could this be a sign of depression?' Raphael wonders. Raphael suddenly thinks of Stephanie. As much as he was initially a bit skeptical about music therapy, now he starts to consider it. Last year, Raphael witnessed first-hand the power of music during André's concerts. Also, how the North Koreans reacted after Stephanie played the violin. It had a huge impact. Music really affects mood and well-being, including mental health. Yeah. Maybe it's time to bring Stephanie in for her expertise.

@@@

"You mean, your André is André Gauthier-Lee? That famous pianist?" Stephanie is shocked. Gaby nods shyly. Stephanie, Gaby, and Michelle are in the middle of their night swim in the hotel's giant pool. The pool is adjacent to the Persian Gulf itself. The atmosphere is very calm with the night lights and the wave sound from the beach.

"It's weird, right? We think we will recognize famous people easily if they pass by us. But it's not always the case," Gaby says.

As a musician herself, Stephanie knows André Gauthier-Lee. He is a piano prodigy and a world-class pianist. But she never really attends his concert in person because the tickets used to be very expensive and always sold out fast. And she is more willing to spend money on violin recitals than piano.

But she wouldn't expect that Raphael's best friend is André Gauthier-Lee himself. Raphael only said that André is a firm owner, not a famous ex-pianist. Stephanie is aware that André has retired due to his health condition.

Earlier, Gaby and Michelle were recounting their love story with André and Guillaume respectively. How Gaby has always been a big fan of André and she decided to follow him to Singapore, Auckland, Geneva, and New York to watch his last concerts. Then they met in Singapore and André accidentally heard Gaby play the piano and invited her to perform with him on stage in Auckland, Geneva, and New York. Then, they fell in love. What a fairytale!

They also met Guillaume in Singapore as Guillaume was André's manager at that time. But Michelle and Guillaume started to fall in love in Geneva. What are the chances that best friends like André and Guillaume fall in love with the Zhang sisters?

"So, how's André after retirement?" Stephanie asks.

It takes some times before Gaby answers, "He's okay. The heart surgery went well and he was recovering well. Raphael said that he has beaten the odds. He was very lucky to be alive. Now he is okay. Maybe a bit depressed and anxious from time to time. But what can we expect? Heart surgery is a major life event," Gaby says.

"Yeah, that's true. Is he still playing the piano?"

"Not that much." Gaby's shoulders slump.

"That's sad. I have listened to him on YouTube before. He is very good."

"Yes, he is. By the way, Steph, Guillaume told me that you are a good swimmer. Maybe you can encourage André to swim again. He used to swim a lot to release stress. Now, he doesn't want to do it because of his surgery scar. As a result, he has no channel to release his stress. Piano and swimming are no longer appealing for him," Gaby adds.

Now Stephanie starts to see these people in a new light. She thought André was just a rich guy without struggles. Apparently, nobody has a perfect life. Maybe Guillaume has his own problems, too. Maybe Raphael, too.

Meanwhile, the more she spends time getting to know Gaby and Michelle, the more she likes them. They took the initiative to invite her for a girls' night swim like this. The three of them have common interests in music, arts, as well as Korean culture. Gaby is a first-year classical piano student, Michelle is a ballet dancer, and Stephanie herself is a music therapist. The three of them also like K-pop and K-dramas. Moreover, Gaby and Michelle are also very open to her and not hesitating to discuss private matters like she is part of the family, too.

"Yeah, I can invite him for a swim tomorrow," Stephanie says.

Michelle looks very enthusiastic now. "Great! None of us, Guillaume, Raphael, Gaby and I, are competitive swimmers like André."

Gaby's face lightens up. "Thanks, Steph. You know, I am very happy that Raphael met you. You are different from most girls he dated in the past," Gaby says.

"Yes, I like this new version of my brother since he met you," Michelle adds.

"What do you mean by new version?" Stephanie asks.

"Before, you left him alone for five minutes, he would already have flirted with the first girl that he saw. Now I see the more serious side of him. Especially when he is with you. He appears more protective than usual," Michelle replies.

Stephanie feels her face heat up and warmth spreads all over her body. She realizes she may have developed feelings towards Raphael herself.

Chapter 14

Dubai, Day 3

This morning, Raphael, Stephanie, and Guillaume work out in the gym. Although Guillaume worked out yesterday, he is still in full stamina today. Stephanie, too, although she is on her period. Raphael doesn't understand how she does that. But he feels motivated working out with them. They do all sorts of compound exercise.

"Do you think André is up for swimming?" Stephanie asks Raphael and Guillaume on the way back to their suite after gym.

"Ah, Michelle told me last night that they told you about what happened to André. Hmm.. I know he hasn't been swimming for a long time. But you can try," Guillaume says.

"But you've just worked out, Steph. Do you still have the energy to swim?" Raphael asks.

"Yes, I do. For me, swimming doesn't take that much effort."

Once they arrive at their suite, they find André, Gaby, and Michelle doing their own activities. André is working, Gaby is reading, and Michelle is practicing her ballet routine.

Stephanie doesn't waste a minute. She walks straight to André.

"Hey, André, everybody told me that you are a swimmer. Wanna do some laps with me this afternoon?"

André looks surprised by her straightforward invitation. He hesitates for a second. Then he realizes that everybody in the room is looking at him, waiting for his response.

He takes a deep breath before answering.

"Sure."

Before André and Stephanie enter the pool, Raphael takes out a bottle of sunscreen. The last thing he wants is for both of them to get sunburn.

"Gabs, take some of this and apply it to André." Raphael puts some sunscreen on Gaby's hand.

"Steph, come here." Raphael motions to Stephanie to sit in front of him on the beach chair. "I will help apply this sunscreen on your back."

"Oh, thanks." She sits with her back towards him.

Although her swimsuit is like the ones that the female Olympic swimmers wear, the back part is mostly bare. Raphael tries to control his thoughts when applying the sunscreen to her back. Most of the women in the pool are wearing bikinis. Before, he thought bikinis were the sexiest swimsuits for women, but now, he finds Stephanie very sexy in her athletic swimsuit. It accentuates her muscular and fit body.

"Ready?" André approaches Stephanie.

"Yes." Stephanie gets up after Raphael finishes applying the sunscreen.

Raphael takes a quick glance at André's scar. His scar from the sternotomy is healing well. It is now appearing as a white line, but is still easily noticeable from two feet away. Luckily, the hair on his chest also starts to grow back and it somewhat hides the scar.

"The length of the pool is about fifty metres. Wanna do a one hundred metres freestyle first?" André asks.

"I'd love that," Stephanie says enthusiastically.

After a quick warm up, they both jump to the pool and start racing. Stephanie and André swim like real Olympians. A lot of people in the swimming pool even clear the way for André and Stephanie. Most of the time, André is slightly faster than Stephanie, but only by a few seconds.

Raphael becomes more and more intrigued by Stephanie. Who is this girl? First, she worked out this morning with him and

Guillaume. Now she still has the energy to race with André. Plus, she is on her period. Even Guillaume is already falling asleep on the beach chair next to him. Michelle is also tired after her ballet practice and has no energy to swim. Is Stephanie human?

Gaby takes a seat beside him.

"I see that you cannot take your eyes off Stephanie." Gaby smiles.

"Is it that obvious?"

"Yes. And I am very happy. She is such a great woman. Yesterday Michelle and I had a great talk with her. And I told her about André. Now look at what she does. This is the first time I see André swim again."

"I know, right. She is very different from other girls that I met. She is very inspiring and strong. Wait until you hear her play the violin. You will be impressed." Raphael sounds very proud.

"Okay, now you sound like me last year. Falling in love with someone after listening to their music," Gaby says.

"I told you. I am passionate about classical music now." "Okay. I believe you."

"André told me he doesn't play piano that often anymore. Does it bother you?"

"I am a bit disappointed. Yes. But I still love him a lot regardless of whether he plays the piano or not. Maybe Stephanie can make André fall in love with piano again!" Gaby is very cheerful now.

"Yes, I think André may benefit from music therapy. I will talk to Steph after."

An hour later, Stephanie and André get out of the pool. They both look very fresh after swimming.

"How is it? Are you guys done?" Raphael asks.

"It's really fun. We are only taking a break. After that we will do a two hundred metres medley, and then finish." André says.

"Okay. As long as you don't overexert yourself," Raphael says.

"Raphael, why don't you join us? Are you good at swimming?" Stephanie asks.

Raphael doesn't answer right away. He enjoys watching people swim. However, when he imagines himself in the swimming pool, his stomach starts to feel uneasy.

"No, I don't, unfortunately. This is the thing I admit I can't do," Raphael replies.

"There is nothing wrong with that. I can't wait for skydiving tomorrow. That's your time to shine." Stephanie throws a sympathetic smile that melts his heart.

@@@

Stephanie starts to like her vacation in Dubai. Today, they do more sports than luxurious stuff. Finally, she feels "normal" again.

She reflects on her day while in the bathroom, drying her hair after a shower. She really enjoyed her swim with André today. If Guillaume is her gym buddy, André is her new swimming buddy. He seemed to enjoy the swim today too despite some people staring at his scar when they stood close by. By the time they did more laps, he appeared more comfortable and cared less about others.

What about Raphael? She admits that she hopes Raphael and her can be more than just a workout buddy. Today she witnessed how he really is such a caring person. After she and André finished their medley swimming—fifty metres for each butterfly, backstroke, breaststroke, and freestyle—André seemed to be out of breath and Raphael quickly pulled him out of the pool. After swimming, Raphael also made sure she ate iron-rich food as she is still on her period.

Once they returned to their suite, Raphael pulled her aside to talk about the possibility of music therapy for André. She remembers when they first met in the ER, Raphael seemed a bit skeptical about music therapy. But now he seems to be open to it.

Actually, Stephanie has thought about it even before Raphael asked. She would not take André as a client, as she doesn't want to mix her personal and professional life, but she can introduce music therapy to him. Or she can refer him to one of her music therapy friends. Usually when she takes a new client, she has to do a lengthy and comprehensive assessment with regards to the clients' physical and mental health and then determine the goal of the therapy and how many sessions would be needed. This will include private and sensitive information that will be awkward to share between friends.

After she finishes drying her hair, she walks out from the bedroom and walk towards the kitchen to get some water. When she passes the living room on the way to the kitchen, Raphael, Guillaume, André, Gaby, and Michelle are all sitting on the couch chatting.

"There you are, Steph," Raphael says.

"Come and sit with us." Gaby moves to the side to give Stephanie a space to sit between her and Raphael. So, Stephanie sits between Gaby and Raphael. Her heart flutters a bit when her arm brushes against Raphael. Raphael wears his usual checkered shirt. He looks very handsome!

"So, Steph, I heard that you are good at playing the violin," Guillaume says.

"I'm just decent, I guess."

Raphael shakes his head. "You are too modest. Otherwise, Mr. Kim wouldn't have asked you to play and you would have been executed," he adds.

Gaby sits straighter, "Can you play something for us? It's not fair that only Raphael has heard you play," she says enthusiastically.

"Umm. Okay. Let me get my violin." Stephanie walks towards her bedroom to get the complimentary violin she got from North Korea.

"What do you want me to play?" Stephanie asks after she returns to the living room. She takes out the violin and starts to tune it.

"How about anything that you feel like playing at this moment," André suggests.

Stephanie thinks for some time before deciding on a piece that she thinks is suitable for her mood at this moment.

"And please stand. Don't be shy." Michelle smiles.

She stands up and starts playing her violin.

The music is with allegro tempo. It starts with a lively and cheerful melody. However, soon after, it becomes dramatic and thrilling. But in the middle of the suspenseful section, there is a hint of humor in it. The music is very unique. Towards the end, it is back to the initial lively and cheerful melody but with more spirit.

After Stephanie finishes playing, everybody claps enthusiastically.

Guillaume comments first, "Wow, Steph. That's really something! Now I understand why the North Koreans asked you to play." He clearly looks impressed.

"I agree," Gaby says.

"I told ya," Raphael says. He is looking at Stephanie proudly as always. Stephanie starts to blush.

Guillaume takes out his business card from his wallet. "I don't know if Raphael has told you, but I am an artist manager for classical musicians. If you ever decide to change your career to become a professional violinist, please contact me," Guillaume says.

"Thank you for the appreciation." Stephanie receives Guillaume's business card although she knows that she is not interested in becoming a professional violinist. She loves being a music therapist.

André, who seemed to be transported to a different world throughout her performance, comes back from his trance. "I really like your playing. This is the first time I heard this piece, though. Who is the composer?" He asks.

Stephanie hesitates for a second.

"Actually, it's me who composed it."

Everybody is even more impressed with this revelation.

Michelle's eyes widen, "Wow. I don't know that you are also a composer in addition to a music therapist!"

"I don't compose often. But yeah, sometimes I cannot find a perfect piece that represents how I feel, so I decide to compose the music myself."

"What's the name of this piece?" Raphael asks.

Stephanie hesitates again. "I will tell you, but don't laugh, okay? Especially you."

"Okay. Tell me. I am curious now," Raphael says.

"It's Epinephrine."

@@@

Raphael cannot stop watching Stephanie who is already falling asleep right after they return to their bedroom. Today was a long day full of exercise for her. She must be very tired. And tomorrow they are going skydiving! He has always been going skydiving by himself because nobody wanted to go with him. For the past few years, he has imagined that someday, there will be someone special who would want to share the adventure with him, including skydiving. Now it seems that he has found that person.

He adjusts Stephanie's blanket gently to avoid waking her up. She looks very peaceful but vulnerable at the same time when sleeping like this.

Raphael is still playing the melody of "Epinephrine" in his head. Now he understands more what she feels inside. She likes adventure. She embraces it. Sometimes it is dramatic and thrilling like what they experienced in North Korea. But after that, this adventure makes her feel more alive and joyful than before. Just like how he feels about it, too. It's very rare that he finds someone in the same tune as him.

Could Stephanie be the woman he is looking for? He likes that she is very independent and not clingy to him like other girls. She gets along very well with his sisters and best friends. Stephanie and he don't need to spend the whole time together, although he feels like he is the one who needs more one-on-one time with her.

In the past whenever he dated a girl, it didn't work out well because of his work schedule. When he has a twelve-hour night shift, obviously he has to sleep during the day. This kind of schedule is very hard for dating. But with someone like Stephanie, he is sure she wouldn't mind. Does he start thinking about dating her?

Chapter 15

Dubai, Day 4

Stephanie has been waiting for this day. The skydiving day. She thought she would be excited, but apparently, she is nervous as hell.

They are scheduled to jump at two p.m. Now it is only eight a.m., and she is already pacing back and front in her room due to nervousness.

Suddenly the door opens and Raphael enters. He already looks fresh and clean with a navy-blue polo shirt and khaki pants. When did he even wake up? Every time Stephanie wakes up, usually Raphael has already left the bed. Either to study for his exam in the living room or to have a morning coffee.

"Hi, Steph. Are you excited for today?" Raphael grins at her. He doesn't look nervous at all.

"I am. But honestly, I am nervous, too."

"It's normal to be nervous, especially for the first time. Let me ask you this, do you think you are in a good shape for skydiving? Is there any medical condition that I am not aware of?" Raphael makes sure.

"Nope. I'm perfectly healthy to go skydiving."

"Great."

"But what if the parachute doesn't open?"

"Then there will be a reserve parachute that will automatically open at a certain altitude."

"Is it scary to free fall? Am I going to feel the stomach-drop sensation?"

"No, you won't. Within a couple of seconds, you will reach a terminal velocity and you will feel like flying." He looks through the window and continues, "Also, the sky is clear today. It's perfect for skydiving. At one point, I was skydiving in the cloudy sky; I could see how fast we dropped from the clouds. But when the sky is clear like this, you won't really notice that you are actually falling."

His comments don't make her feel better.

"How many times have you done this before?"

"Four times. One in Golden, BC, one in Cayuga, Ontario, one in Niagara Falls, and one in Montreal. It's very addicting. And the view is incredible."

"Okay."

"Let's eat breakfast first." Raphael grabs her hand.

They arrive at the skydiving center forty minutes before they are scheduled to jump. Upon arrival, they sign a waiver form that basically says that if something wrong happens to them, they won't sue. This doesn't make Stephanie feel better at all. She feels like throwing up her breakfast, scramble eggs and toast with apple jam.

Raphael keeps squeezing her hand to reassure her.

"You look a bit pale, Steph. Are you sure you are okay?"

"I'm okay. I'm a bit nervous. But it's normal, as you said."

"Listen, I know that this is my idea. But you can cancel at any time if you don't feel comfortable."

"No, no. I won't cancel. I will continue."

"Okay. The first jump is always the hardest. After that, either you will like it or you will hate it. But knowing you, I'm sure that you will like it."

"I believe you," she says, although she is still unsure. "Is there anything you are afraid to do, Raphael? You seem to be fearless in everything."

"Everybody has their own fear. Including me."

Raphael doesn't explain further. So, Stephanie doesn't want to probe.

Fifteen minutes before their jump, they meet the instructors who will do the tandem jump with them. They are also briefed about the jump position and the landing position. There are two possible drop zones, the palm drop zone or the desert zone. They picked the palm drop zone as it is closer to Palm Jumeirah where they are staying and it offers the incredible view of Palm Jumeirah itself.

Then, the instructors put a harness on them. Now their shoulders, chest, back, hips, and thighs feel heavy with the harness. After that, they walk towards the plane that is waiting for them outside the hangar.

Stephanie is wondering, what if she refuses to jump by the time they are up there? Will they push her? Of course she is not going to stop at this point. She has paid quite a lot for this.

They enter the plane, which is similar to a small military plane that can only fit no more than ten people. There is no seat as well.

Their plane finally takes off.

Inside the plane, the instructor attaches his harness to Stephanie's. Raphael's instructor does the same. So now they are stuck with their tandem instructors together until they land. But what if the harness doesn't attach properly and she free-falls without her instructor and without a parachute? Stephanie tries to get rid of that thought. Honestly, Raphael's presence gives a huge comfort for her. If she did this by herself, she probably would have cried already.

"Steph, if you are nervous, just play 'Epinephrine' in your head," Raphael says. Ah, good idea. Stephanie nods. In her head, she tries to play the melody that she created. Their adrenaline hormone is going to start kicking in shortly, or it may have already started. Stephanie tries to take it lightly and finds a sense of humor in all of this.

The higher the plane goes up, the more beautiful the view is. And the sky is clear. Thank God. So, they won't feel that they are falling, according to Raphael's explanation this morning.

At twelve thousand feet, the plane finally is slowing down and hovering around.

The instructors tell them to put on the goggles and then one of them opens the plane's door.

Stephanie feels her heartbeats accelerate. Wow. This is the first time she is flying in a plane with the door opened. The wind sound from outside is really intimidating. Are they really going to jump just like that?

Raphael and his instructor approach the opened door first.

"I'll see you soon, Steph!" Raphael says when he is at the door about to jump. After that, he and his instructor jump first without hesitation. He even lets out a cry of excitement. It kind of gives her a slight encouragement.

Then Stephanie and her instructor step towards the opened door.

"Ready to jump?" her instructor asks.

"Yes." She nods.

Stephanie takes a deep breath and jumps from the plane into thin air.

Wow.

Raphael is right. She doesn't feel like falling. She feels like flying!

She positions her body like an arch like how she has been instructed during the briefing. The Palm Jumeirah below her looked small from the plane a few seconds ago, and suddenly it becomes bigger and closer right away. That shows that she is actually falling extremely fast. The wind from below pushes her body up and so she feels like she is flying steadily instead of falling.

And the view below is really breathtaking. Aside from the Palm Jumeirah, she can see the Persian Gulf as well as the Dubai skylines. This is definitely an incredible experience.

"Look, your friend is there. Do you want to come closer to him?" her instructor asks while they are still freefalling.

"Yes, sure," Stephanie says to her instructor. After that, they "fly" towards Raphael and his instructor.

Raphael and his instructor also try to fly closer to them. After they are close enough, Raphael reaches out his hand towards her and she tries to grab it. They can only grab each other's hand for a few seconds before the wind separates them.

After about one minute of freefall, she can feel that her parachute opens. It initially pulls her body a few meters up, but after that, she finds herself in a comfortable sitting position.

She sees that Raphael's parachute has also opened and now they are dropping to the ground at a slower pace. He waves at her with a big smile.

"How do you like it, Steph?" Raphael has to shout as the wind is still pretty loud. Their positions are further from each other now after the parachute opens.

"I love it! It's incredible!" she shouts back with two thumbs up.

"Great!"

After that, Raphael's instructor lets him maneuver their parachute towards the landing zone. Stephanie and her instructor wait a few more minutes before following their directions.

They are getting closer and closer to the ground now. Her instructor told her to be ready for landing. She lifts both of her legs straightforwardly as instructed during the briefing.

A few minutes later, they land on their bum smoothly on the grass. Raphael has landed a few meters in front of her.

By the time Stephanie finishes releasing herself from her harness, Raphael is already standing in front of her. She doesn't waste a single second. Her body is full of adrenaline.

She throws herself towards Raphael. She hugs him because she feels so grateful that he introduces her to this new experience. She cannot stop smiling.

Raphael hugs her back tightly. Not only hug, he also lowers his lips to meet hers.

She can feel his heart beating very fast. It's definitely more than one hundred bpm. She is sure that her heartbeat is not slower than his.

They kiss each other passionately.

After an intense experience, they don't care about their surroundings. Stephanie feels like she finally finds someone whom she has been looking for all this time. Someone who shares her adventurous spirit. Someone who opens her world and she opens his. Someone with whom she can be herself but she still feels appreciated and loved.

That someone is standing in front of her and expressing his love to her.

Her body feels warm and she feels very comfortable in his hug. She never knew that loving the right person can feel rewarding and fulfilling. She wishes she could stop the time right now and hug and kiss Raphael forever.

Stephanie doesn't know how long their hug and kiss last. The next thing she knows is they lay down on the grass side by side, catching their breaths and looking at the blue sky where they have just been a few minutes ago.

"Now I know what you are talking about. I feel like I can conquer everything after jumping out of the plane," Stephanie says.

"I know, right. Thank you for coming with me, Steph," Raphael says while still looking at the sky.

"Thank you for bringing me here, Raphael. I really enjoyed it."

"You are the first woman who is willing to go skydiving with me. I feel like I finally found someone who is in the same rhythm as me." Raphael is now resting on his elbow, looking at her in the eyes.

"Me, too."

"How about we continue our adventure in a quieter place?"

"Like where?" Now Stephanie is also resting on her elbow and facing Raphael.

"I always want to go to a Kibbutz in Israel. Maybe the ones around Lake Galilee. We can enjoy a more nature-oriented vacation there."

"That sounds like a great idea. Actually, there is a hike that I did once in Israel. The trail started from Nazareth and ended up in Capernaum. But it's sixty-five km though. I think I want to do it again. Do you want to join me?" Stephanie asks.

It doesn't take long for Raphael to reply. "This is definitely what I am looking for! Sixty-five kilometres. Wow. It also sounds more natural than here. I am kind of tired of Dubai and all its luxury, to be honest," Raphael says. "But you don't mind repeating the hike?"

"Not at all." A couple years ago, she did this hike alone. Back then, she imagined that someday she would want to do that long hike again, but with someone special to her. Now it seems that she has found that person. But she is too shy to admit it.

"Alright, then. Let's go!" Raphael gets up and helps Stephanie to stand. He suddenly looks very enthusiastic. And so does she.

@@@

Raphael cannot imagine a better day than today.

Now he is sitting with Stephanie, Gaby, Michelle, André, and Guillaume in the lounge beside the hotel's pool to celebrate their final night in Dubai. He has informed the group that he and Stephanie have decided to fly to Israel tomorrow. It turns out that André, Guillaume, Gaby, and Michelle also agree to leave Dubai. The reason they picked this place in the first place is because none of them has visited Dubai before and here is a great city to have fun with friends. They like the idea of visiting Israel but Michelle prefers to stay in Tel Aviv rather than Galilee. Michelle is more like a city girl than a farm girl. While André, Guillaume, and Gaby are pretty flexible.

As such, the six of them will fly together to Israel tomorrow. However, while André, Guillaume, Gaby, and Michelle will stay in Tel Aviv, Raphael and Stephanie will continue their trip to Nazareth the next day. When Raphael and Stephanie ask the group if anybody wants to join them, they get similar replies to last time.

"Walking and hiking for sixty-five km? Why don't you just take a bus?" Michelle asks.

"You miss the point, Michelle. That's where the fun is, when we walk and hike. Not riding a bus." Raphael says.

"Well, I am a ballet dancer, and my feet are already full of blisters. Hiking sixty-five km is not going to help. I will pass. But have fun, though!"

"I will accompany Michelle," Guillaume says.

"I don't think my cardiologist will approve of this hike. Sorry, I will pass," André says.

"I will accompany André," Gaby says.

"Okay. It's just me and Steph, then," Raphael says. And he doesn't mind at all. He is looking forward to spending one-on-one time with Stephanie. His sisters and his friends also probably want to let him and Stephanie have a more private moment.

After the skydiving, Raphael and Stephanie are no longer shy in expressing their attractions towards each other in front of other people. They become more and more comfortable with each other. Raphael feels like he becomes a teenager again.

"So, what did you guys do while Stephanie and I went skydiving?" Raphael asks the group after he recounted their skydiving experience.

"Michelle and I walked along the beach in the morning. It was pretty nice. After that Michelle went shopping with Gaby," Guillaume answers.

"I helped André reviewing some financial statements of the company that he is going to invest in before I went shopping. At least my accounting skills are still valuable," Gaby says.

"Yes, very much. I relied a lot on Gaby's analysis sometimes. It saved me a lot of time." André pats Gaby's head gently as a gesture of being proud. Raphael likes seeing the teamwork between André and Gaby. As an ex-pianist, now André is helping Gaby with her piano studies. As an ex-CPA, now Gaby is helping André with Gauthier Capital, the private equity firm that André owns.

"Oh, and André also spent quite some time on the piano in the conference room after work." Gaby smiles.

"Oh, really? You play piano again? What do you play?" Stephanie asks.

"I will show you guys later." André smiles mysteriously.

"And what did you guys buy from shopping? Branded clothes? Handbags?" Raphael asks Michelle and Gaby.

"No. It's also a secret," Michelle says.

"Why is everybody full of secrets today?" Raphael pouts.

It's nine p.m. but they still want to chill and chat in the lounge, so Raphael walks towards the bar to order more drinks. There are a bunch of drunken male teenagers by the bar. They are surrounded by female teenagers who also appear to be drunk.

When the bartender gives him the drinks, one of the drunken teenagers moves his arm blindly and accidentally topples Raphael's drinks to the floor.

"Watch out, man." Raphael is irritated. The drunken guy turns towards him and looks at him up and down.

"Relax, *chink*. It's just a drink." Then he turns away to face the girl he was talking to before he drops Raphael's drink.

Raphael's body is boiling. He tries to remain calm. This is not the first time someone threw him a racist comment.

"What did you just say?"

Now the drunken guy turns his body and looks at him intensely. "I said it's just a drink, *chink*." He repeats with a provoking tone. He is waiting for Raphael to react. His friends also start taking interest in this scene.

It's not worth it. They are just childish and drunk. Raphael says to himself. He ignores the drunken teenager and orders another drink from the bar.

"Hey *chink*, it is true that you have a small package?" The second drunken guy provokes him. His comments make the people in his group laugh.

"You have some growing up to do, kids," Raphael replies calmly. The second guy seems frustrated that the insult doesn't seem to trigger his reaction.

Raphael is about to leave the bar when the second guy suddenly punches his fist towards Raphael's face.

He didn't expect this. He loses balance slightly but quickly steadies himself. His face feels hot now, as well as his entire body. He can feel that blood starts dripping from his nose. He hopes it's not broken. As much as he wants to punch this guy back, he restrains himself. His job is to save life, not to cause harm. He will let it slide this time.

He walks away again, but these guys don't stop. Now the first guy tries to punch him, but this time, he is ready. Raphael avoids his fist, and as a result, the first guy loses balance and falls to the floor instead.

This humiliation makes them become more aggressive. Two other guys grab both of Raphael's arms and the first guy can now punch him freely in the stomach.

Raphael feels an intense pain, both physical and emotional. But the physical pain is nothing compared to the humiliation that he has to endure.

"Stop it!" He suddenly hears Guillaume's voice. He looks up and finds Guillaume, André, Stephanie, Gaby, and Michelle standing there. He never sees Guillaume that angry before. He wishes he could vanish. He doesn't want to show weakness, especially in front of Stephanie.

Guillaume punches the first guy in the face. The second guy tries to punch Guillaume as revenge for his friend but André stops him by throwing his body against him. Now both André and the second guy are dueling on the floor.

The guys that are still holding Raphael can sense that Raphael's friends are stronger than their friends. By the time Raphael regains his strength, the trio can probably defeat the four attackers. So, both of them push Raphael hard until he falls backwards.

Unfortunately, the swimming pool is right behind him, and he falls right into the swimming pool.

@@@

It's Gaby and Michelle's scream that wakes Stephanie up.

Everything happened so fast. As much as Stephanie wants to help since she arrived at the scene, she knows that as a woman, she is not a match for these guys, no matter how tom-boy she is. So, she lets Guillaume and André take care of them.

But when two guys pushed Raphael to the pool, she felt very angry and she started walking towards those two guys. She didn't have a plan yet, maybe to push them both to the pool, too. Until she heard Gaby screaming, "No!!"

Everybody is looking at Gaby now. "Raphael... Raphael cannot swim." Gaby and Michelle start running towards the pool to save Raphael. André, who is in the middle of dueling with the second guy, looks at the swimming pool with horror.

"Stay back!" André shouts at Gaby and Michelle. He quickly abandons the duel, and jumps into the pool immediately.

Stephanie looks at the pool. She expects Raphael's head to have emerged from the pool, but it hasn't. No way, he is not drowning, is he?

Without thinking, she switches her direction to follow André and jumps into the pool herself.

By the time she joins André and Raphael in the pool, André has managed to secure Raphael's head above the water. Raphael is choking and gasping for air. Luckily, he is not unconscious.

Stephanie helps André carry Raphael towards the edge of the pool. André gets out of the pool and skillfully pulls Raphael out from the pool with her help.

Outside of the pool, Raphael keeps coughing and vomiting water—and blood.

"Call 911, quick." Michelle is panicking from the sight of blood. Gaby starts to cry beside her.

"No," Raphael says with a weak and hoarse voice. He is still trying to breathe.

"What do you mean no? You are bleeding," Michelle says.

"It's not... from my lungs, it's from... my nose."

Stephanie, who now has come out from the pool, looks at Raphael's face in more detail. His nose is swollen and she sees a trace of blood. She wants to cry like Gaby at this point.

"Raphael, tell us what we need to do to help you." André's voice is trembling. Raphael, André, and Stephanie are now shivering in their wet clothes.

"Let me catch...my breath...first." Raphael is surprisingly very calm after a near drowning experience. How is this possible?

Meanwhile, Guillaume finishes fighting with those drunken guys. He only got a split lip. Some security personnel have arrived to take control of the situation. They keep those drunken teenagers away from Raphael's team.

One of the security approaches Raphael.

"Are you okay? Do you need to go to the hospital?"

"No."

Raphael tries to gather himself and gets up, but he almost loses balance before André and Stephanie support him. He winces in pain.

"Let me sit... a little longer." Raphael sits back on the ground and puts his head between his knees.

"Take your time, Raphael," André says.

"In the meantime... are you guys... okay? Any injuries?" Raphael asks.

"Stop worrying about us and worry about yourself," Guillaume says. "I wish I could beat them up more." He looks angrier than Raphael.

A few minutes later, Raphael is able to stand on his own. But André and Stephanie insisted on supporting him. At least Raphael doesn't refuse their help this time.

They go up to their suites to clean themselves up.

@@@

"How are you feeling?" Guillaume asks Raphael while they both are alone in Raphael's bathroom. Stephanie is showering in Guillaume and Michelle's room while André is showering in his room. Raphael wishes he can be by himself, but Guillaume insists on helping him.

"I am okay. How about you?" He notices that Guillaume's bottom lip is split and his jaw starts to swell. But other than that, he looks okay.

"I am okay, too. Better than you for sure," Guillaume replies.

Raphael looks at himself in the bathroom's mirror. He looks like a mess. His nose hurts and is swollen but at least no broken bones. The bleeding has stopped, too.

Raphael removes his shirt and examines the spot where he got hit. Luckily, there is no organ damage, although his abdomen still feels stiff. He takes a deep breath to ensure that there is no fluid left in his lungs. He feels grateful that André and Stephanie pulled him out of the water quickly; otherwise, he cannot imagine the damage his lungs or brain may sustain. His shirt is stained with blood from his nose, so he starts washing it in the sink.

Guillaume takes his bloody shirt. "I will wash this. Remove your remaining clothes and wash yourself."

"Thanks, Guillaume." Raphael removes his pants and he is about to remove his boxers when he remembers one of the drunken guys' comments about the "small package".

He is boiling again. He knows that he has a normal size despite being an Asian man. But that comment really bothers him.

"Guillaume, I think I can shower on my own." Raphael hopes he picks up the cue.

"Sure, I am done washing your shirt anyway. Shout if you need any help, okay? And don't faint, please. I won't know what to do." Guillaume says and then leaves. Raphael likes that Guillaume is always chill and can always turn every situation into a humorous one.

He doesn't think that he is going to faint, although he feels a bit dizzy and weak after the beating and the near-drowning experience. He is also still shivering. But he knows that right now, his body is still full of adrenaline. Once the hormones wear off, he may feel even worse.

Raphael sighs and steps into the shower.

Chapter 16

Dubai, Day 5

Stephanie cannot sleep, and she keeps glancing at Raphael, who sleeps on the other bed. He looks asleep but Stephanie doesn't know if he is really asleep or not. There is something that doesn't add up. She feels that something is wrong. There is something that Raphael is hiding.

Earlier after everybody had finished cleaning up themselves, they gathered in Raphael's and her bedroom. Raphael has showered and has put on clean clothes. He looked pale, but other than his nose, it didn't look like he sustained any other serious injury. Raphael even took care of Guillaume's split lip and gave him an ice pack for his swollen jaw. André looked a bit shaken but he didn't sustain any injury.

Raphael quickly told them what actually happened before those drunken guys started punching him, including when they called him *chink*. Stephanie felt very angry for him. Although Raphael recounted the story casually like it was not a big deal, she thought that he was just putting on a brave face.

"Did you punch them back at all, to protect yourself?" André asked Raphael.

"Well, no. You know what the bible says, when someone slaps your right cheek, give your left cheek, or something along that line."

Guillaume sighs impatiently, "Are you kidding me, Raphael? I know you don't want to hurt people because it contradicts your profession, but you are entitled to defend yourself!"

Michelle steps in too, "And I know you are strong enough to defeat them."

"Actually, I am not sure. There were four of them. I was outnumbered until you guys came to rescue me." Raphael smiled calmly.

Stephanie tried to defend Raphael. "Raphael is right. Especially when they were drunk. It's better not to provoke them even more."

Gaby jumps in, "In any case, I am glad that you are okay now, Raphael. I was so scared earlier. Let us know if you don't feel well, okay?" Her voice is full of worries.

"I will. Thanks, Gabs. Let's sleep, guys. We have a flight to catch tomorrow."

Stephanie has known Raphael for quite some time now. There is something off with him since he was rescued from the pool. But she cannot pinpoint what it is and Raphael hasn't discussed anything else with her other than what he has shared with his sisters and his friends. At this point, she will just wait until Raphael opens up.

She closes her eyes and tries to sleep.

She must have fallen asleep when she heard Raphael's scream on the other bed.

Her heart stops for a second.

She quickly jumps from her bed and runs towards his bed.

It seems like Raphael is having a nightmare. He starts gasping for air and hyperventilating. His whole body is also shaking. With his eyes still closed, he is pulling the t-shirt fabric around the neck as if he is suffocated. His face is full of sweat and his t-shirt is damp.

"Raphael, wake up. It's just a bad dream." Stephanie shakes his arm gently. His skin feels cold and clammy. Raphael continues to writhe. He seems to be in agony.

Stephanie continues trying to wake him up. Seeing him like this scares her, too.

"Raphael, you are going to be okay. Take a deep breathe." She holds his hand and whispers gently into his ear.

Finally, he wakes up. He is choking and disoriented at first.

Still suffocated, Raphael looks at her and sits up. He is breathing hard and his face is still full of horror.

"I..." He doesn't finish his sentence and instead he gets up from the bed and scrambles towards the bathroom. Stephanie follows him panicky.

In the bathroom, she finds him kneeling in front of the toilet and throwing up in there. He seems really sick. Is this because of the nightmare or the near-drowning incident that he had earlier? Or is this because of the punch to his stomach? She looks at the vomit in the toilet and feels relieved when there is no blood in it.

Stephanie pats his back gently while he continues throwing up. She finds herself also shaking, as she is scared seeing him like this.

"Steph... you shouldn't... be here." Raphael tries to catch his breath. He wipes his mouth with the back of his hand. After that he flushes the toilet.

"I want to be here. Tell me what you need."

Raphael doesn't answer. He stands up wobbly and walks to the sink to wash his face and his hands. He must feel awful after throwing up.

After that he sits on the bathroom floor with his back against the wall. He closes his eyes while regulating his breathing.

"I am sorry that you have to witness this. I tend to vomit when I am stressed. Gaby and my mom, too. It runs in the family," Raphael says.

"It's okay. Everybody vomits from time to time. But let me take care of you, Raphael." Stephanie feels her eyes start tearing up, too. She also doesn't want Raphael to see this. So, she gets up and walks to the bedroom to grab a dry t-shirt for him as an excuse. She wipes her eyes before returning to the bathroom.

"You need to change, otherwise you can get sicker." She offers him the t-shirt.

"Thanks." He changes his t-shirt quickly. She is relieved when she finds no visible bruises on his body. For now, she assumes that his vomiting and labored breathing had nothing to do with the injury from the fight earlier. It is likely related to his nightmare, which could be related to the incident.

Raphael wraps his arms around his knees and buries his face in them.

She just sits beside him on the floor without making a sound. She lets him gather himself. She won't push him to talk if he doesn't want to. She just wants to be there for him.

Raphael is still not talking for the next fifteen minutes. At one point, Stephanie gets up to grab water from the kitchen and lets him drink. He must be dehydrated after vomiting and sweating. After that they continue to sit in silence.

"Now you know that I am not as fearless as you thought." Raphael finally starts talking.

"What do you mean?"

"Something happened to me when I was eight years old. Do you want to hear?"

"Yes, of course."

It was lunchtime at school, he was sitting by himself in a cafeteria, reading an encyclopedia for children about the human brain. His father just gave it to him yesterday as his birthday gift. Now he couldn't stop reading. He was too absorbed.

Suddenly a group of older guys snatched the book from him. He was surprised. He didn't even realize that they were coming.

"Give it back, please," he said to the gang. They were just laughing at him. Why were they always targeting him? Was it because he is Asian? What's the difference? Was it just because of the skin color? He spoke English perfectly like all of them without an accent. Why did they always treat him differently?

The gang took his book outside of the cafeteria. He chased them until they were in the playground.

"Give me back my book," Raphael repeated.

"Say it in Chinese," one of the boys said.

"I don't know how to say it in Chinese. I don't speak Chinese."

"Liar! Liar!" They were laughing at him.

"I was born here. I only speak English."

They kept making fun of him. One of the boys took his glasses and they passed it along to their friends. They called him a Chinese nerd who only knew about studying.

After that, another boy pushed him to the ground and punched him in the stomach. Everybody laughed again. Everything became overwhelming. It was even scarier as he couldn't see clearly without glasses.

The bell suddenly rang and it was time to go back to class.

"What should I do with this?" One of the boys raised the encyclopedia in his hand.

"Throw it in the swimming pool!" one of them suggested. So, the boy who held the encyclopedia did what his friend told him.

Raphael felt more overwhelmed when they threw his encyclopedia to the pool than when they punched him. He didn't want to lose the book. It was so precious to him. His encyclopedia was now under the water and wet. He had to retrieve it.

Ignoring the pain in his stomach, he ran towards the swimming pool to save his encyclopedia. He didn't know how to swim, but he didn't care. He wanted to finish reading the encyclopedia. His dad would be sad if he lost the encyclopedia. He didn't want to make his dad sad.

So, he jumped towards the pool.

He didn't realize that the pool was deep. His feet couldn't touch the bottom of the pool. And nobody told him that the water burned his eyes. He moved his arms and kicked frantically to emerge to the surface, but to no avail.

The next thing he knew, he struggled to breathe. Every time he breathed, it felt like thousands of knives stabbing his chest.

He didn't know how long he was drowning in the swimming pool. He almost gave up. After that he remembered he was lying down beside the swimming pool. Someone repeatedly pushed his chest and gave him rescue breaths. After that he kept vomiting water. Every time he tried to breathe, his chest felt extremely painful. He was in and out of consciousness.

Then, he found himself waking up in the hospital. It was very uncomfortable as he was hooked to so many wires. But he was so relieved when he saw his family beside him. His mother was always there with the four-year-old Gaby while carrying two-year-old Michelle. She was crying a lot. His father was also there with red and wet eyes.

The first words Raphael said after he was able to speak again were, "Sorry, Dad. I couldn't save the encyclopedia. It was all wet."

"Don't worry about the encyclopedia. As long as you are saved, that's what's important for me."

When he was finally discharged from the hospital, his dad had replaced the encyclopedia with a new one. Not only that, now he had a complete series, not just human brain, but also human respiratory system, digestive system, musculoskeletal system, et cetera.

Although at the end he was saved, the fact that he was bullied because he was "different" would always leave a scar. He also started to develop aversion towards swimming pool. Every time he saw a swimming pool, he would always rewind that bullying scene. His heart started to accelerate, his palms became sweaty, and he started to feel nauseous.

Whenever he looked at Gaby and Michelle, he couldn't imagine if they had to experience what he had experienced. Since then, he became overprotective towards his sisters. Every time Gaby and Michelle asked him why he didn't want to learn how to swim, he told them he almost drowned during his first swimming lesson. He never told them what actually happened to him.

"So that's it. Do you think I am pathetic?" Raphael asks after finishing his story.

"Why pathetic? Carrying a trauma like this throughout your life is not easy. And tonight, your stressor was triggered again in the worst possible way. Of course it will affect you very strongly. And talking it out like this will help. There is nothing to be embarrassed about," she says.

"Yes, but it's hard to admit this fact. Especially in front of a swimmer like you."

"Everybody has weaknesses. You are good at other things, like squash and tennis, for example. Also, you know how to save life. Remember that."

"Thanks, Steph."

She puts her arm around his shoulder.

"Do you really know what I am thinking right now?"

"Yes, tell me."

"I think you are very brave tonight. The fact that you managed to restrain yourself from punching those people who bullied you, it must have required a lot of strength. The fact that you told me your story, it required vulnerability. Never be ashamed of what you are. You are not defined by your race, or your physical strength, or even your profession. You are defined by how well you treat others and how you overcome adversities."

Now she puts his head on her shoulder.

"From now on, you can always be yourself in front of me. You don't need to appear confident, humorous, or strong all the time if that's not how you feel inside."

She can feel that he nods on her shoulder. She continues on.

"Remember what you said to me in Juche Tower? Sometimes it's also good to let other people take care of you. Now let me do that to you."

He sits straighter and looks at her deeply in the eyes. At that moment, she knows that she wants to protect him.

"Thank you, Steph. For everything. For saving my life and for giving me emotional support. You know, I kept replaying your composition, 'Epinephrine', in my head. It helped me control my emotions when they tried to hurt me. It helps me see more humor in it, too. I want to hear more of your violin from now on. I think I need some music therapy." Raphael smiles at her. His smile makes him look very handsome despite his condition at this moment.

"Sure. I can play for you in the morning. For now, you have to sleep. It's already three a.m."

@@@

It's already eight a.m. when Raphael wakes up. He still feels shitty, but at least he feels better than last night. They have a flight to catch at three p.m. today.

He notices that Stephanie has left her bed. He remembers their intimate conversation last night in the bathroom. His heart flutters when thinking about it.

Suddenly he hears a knock on his door.

"Raphael, can I come in?" It's Guillaume.

"Yes."

Guillaume enters the room already fully dressed up elegantly as usual. He looks at Raphael and a worried expression comes across his face right away.

"Hey, are you sick?" Guillaume automatically puts his hand on Raphael's forehead. Raphael quickly shakes his head. "No. I am just tired. What's up?"

"You need to shower and get dressed now. We have a surprise for you."

"What surprise?"

"It's not a surprise if I tell you now. Go get ready. Do you bring any formal or business casual clothes? I am not talking about your usual checkered shirts."

Now he understands why Guillaume and Michelle fell in love with each other. They both are obsessed with dressing up nicely, unlike him.

"Yes, but why do I need to dress up?"

"You will know later. Now go shower." Guillaume orders him and starts going through his luggage to find his clothes. Very respectful, Raphael thinks sarcastically.

But when he looks at his reflection in the bathroom's mirror, he agrees with Guillaume. He looks like a mess. There are dark circles under his eyes. Hopefully by dressing up nicer than usual, he will look less like a mess.

Guillaume takes him to the hotel lobby. Raphael is wearing the suit he wore when visiting Kim Il-Sung and Kim Jong-Il's statue in North Korea.

They arrive in front of a little stage in the lobby that has a grand piano. André is already there in his suit with a woman carrying her violin. Raphael's jaw drops.

"Stephanie??" He cannot believe his eyes. Stephanie looks very different! She is wearing a stunning blue dress that wraps her body until the knees. It has an off-shoulder neckline with little sleeves, which is perfect for her broad shoulder. On top of that, Stephanie is also wearing makeup. It must be Michelle who did that. Her brunette hair falls beautifully in waves on her shoulder.

Last time in North Korea, she looked like a gorgeous noble lady in Hanbok. This time, she looks like a stunning Hollywood actress.

"Hey, Raphael. Have a seat. We will play something for you shortly." Stephanie smiles at him.

He notices that there are four seats in front of the stage. Gaby and Michelle are already sitting there. They wave at him excitedly.

Raphael and Guillaume take a seat beside Gaby and Michelle. This is like a private concert!

André sits behind the piano and Stephanie stands in front of the piano facing the four spectators. A lot of other hotel staff and guests also take interest in this little concert. They are also curious about what André and Stephanie will perform.

Then, André and Stephanie look at each other before starting their music. They draw a sharp breath and the piece starts very dramatic right away.

It's the second movement of Dvorak's Four Romantic Pieces.

Capriccio.

Raphael recognizes the piece right away. He has listened to this music several times after Stephanie told him that these romantic pieces are her favorites.

If the first movement (Cavatina) is calm and soothing, the second movement (Capriccio) is much more intense. The tempo is Allegro maestoso.

Raphael cannot take his eyes off Stephanie. She plays this virtuosic violin piece skillfully and full of emotions. André is also accompanying her synchronically. This piece is like a back-and-forth dialog between intense phrases and playful phrases. It can represent what they all have experienced for the past few days in Dubai. A swimming competition between André and Stephanie, skydiving, and Raphael's incident yesterday. It's intense and thrilling when it happened, but now looking back, there is always something to be appreciated from it. André starts to swim and play piano again and is less depressed; Stephanie now understands how fun skydiving is; and Raphael is grateful to have loyal family and friends who don't hesitate to back him up when he is in trouble.

Then, Stephanie and André end the piece in a way that makes the audience want to hear more. Raphael is waiting for them to play the third movement impatiently.

However, they don't start the third movement. When everybody, including the staff and guests, realizes that Stephanie and André only play one movement, they clap enthusiastically. It was such an impressive and unexpected performance.

Instead of playing the third movement, Stephanie and André play another piano and violin duet.

Raphael had never heard of this piece before.

The piece is another virtuosic piece with allegro tempo. In the beginning, it sounds very industrious and hard to play. But the rhythmical pattern makes this piece sound very cool. Progressively, the music becomes more like a sweet melody, although still with a fast tempo. Towards the end, the melody sounds very rewarding to hear. By the time they finish playing, there is a sense of fulfillment after listening to this piece. This is indeed such a powerful piece, especially with the deep vibrato and progressive dynamics that Stephanie adds.

Everybody claps again, this time with fulfilling emotions.

André and Stephanie bow together towards the audience and they step off the stage.

"Do you like it?" Stephanie approaches him straight.

"I don't like it. I love it. It's incredible, Steph." He hugs her, feeling proud. "But what is the last piece? It sounds very unique but rewarding and fulfilling to hear," Raphael says to her after he releases the hug.

"André, go ahead and tell Raphael," Stephanie says.

André steps closer. "It's my composition. After listening to Steph's composition, I was inspired to start composing again," André says. His eyes are very lively when he says it.

"Tell him the inspiration behind the piece, André," Gaby says encouragingly.

Raphael is staring at André curiously.

André looks a bit shy. "Err... your relationship with Stephanie has inspired me. You guys always do dangerous things that nobody else wants to do. But that's what brings you guys closer together. Then I start to see the love sparks between the two of you. In the end, it's very rewarding to get to know both of you. Raphael, you saved my life last year. Stephanie, you helped me re-discover the part of me that I have forgotten. Raphael, Steph, your passion for adventure, bravery, and heroism has inspired all of us. So, this composition is my gift for both of you. I hope you like it," André explains.

"Wow, André..." Raphael loses his words for a second. He looks at Stephanie, who also appears touched by André's explanation behind his composition.

"So, is this what you did yesterday when Stephanie and I went skydiving? You start composing again. Not just for piano but also for violin?" Raphael asks. That is a huge progress for André.

"Yes." André nods.

Raphael turns towards Gaby and Michelle.

"And the dress that Stephanie is currently wearing, is that what you bought from shopping yesterday?" Gaby and Michelle nod at the same time. They look very happy for Raphael.

"And we hope that this will cheer you up after what happened yesterday," Guillaume adds.

Raphael looks at every one of them. What did he do to deserve these people in his life? He almost becomes emotional.

André turns to Raphael, "And one more thing, can you guess the title of this new piece? I asked Steph already and she guessed it right. Now is your turn."

Raphael already knows since they finish playing the piece.

"It's easy. Dopamine."

André looks impressed.

Chapter 17

Tel Aviv
Israel, Day 1

After a three-hour flight, they finally arrive at Ben Gurion Airport at five p.m. local time.

Guillaume has booked a hotel near Tel Aviv Promenade, which is right by the beach overlooking the Mediterranean Sea. While André, Guillaume, Gaby, and Michelle will stay in Tel Aviv for the next few days, Raphael and Stephanie will stay in Tel Aviv for the first night, and then continue to Nazareth tomorrow morning. After that, they are going to take a long hike to Galilee, which will take three to four days, while staying in local accommodations. They are very excited.

However, for the first night, Raphael and Stephanie will "crash" at the hotel suite that Guillaume has booked. It only has two bedrooms with a king-size bed. As such, the sleeping arrangement will be girls versus boys.

Honestly, Stephanie doesn't mind at all. She thinks that she will have more time with Raphael when they are on their way to Galilee. Tonight, will be a good opportunity to spend time with Gaby and Michelle. As it is almost Christmas now, they have agreed that Israel will be their last destination and after that they all will return to Toronto in early January or even before.

After having supper at the restaurant near the beach, they take a night walk along the promenade. The atmosphere is very relaxing, although Stephanie can't wait to visit a quieter place tomorrow. Tel Aviv is still a metropolitan city after all.

Upon returning to their hotel, Stephanie is now enjoying the girls' night chat with Gaby and Michelle in the bedroom. She hasn't forgotten that Gaby and Michelle bought her that stunning blue dress when she went skydiving with Raphael. She insisted on paying them, but they refused. Michelle also put some makeup on her before her performance in the hotel lobby in Dubai. She really appreciated these kind gestures.

"So how is it going between you and our brother?" Michelle asks.

Stephanie can feel her face start to blush. "It's great. We both are enjoying our adventures together. We are really in the same tune. It's so rare for me to find someone who is similar to me," Stephanie says.

Gaby's face lights up. "I bet it's the same thing for him. Although he used to always flirt here and there, I know that deep down he is still longing for deep and real connection," Gaby says.

"And how far is the physical intimacy between you and Raphael?" Michelle asks bluntly. Stephanie is not expecting this question. But by now, she is aware that in Asian culture, or she should say the "Zhang" culture, they really share everything. It's not because they are nosy, but more because they care.

"Michelle..." Gaby throws Michelle a warning look.

"What? I am not trying to be nosy. Look, Steph, if you have any questions or uncertainties about Raphael, you can always ask us. We will try to help. Say, if there is any cultural barrier that you experience, I can maybe relate to you, as I am dating Guillaume, who comes from a very different cultural background than me."

"Thanks, Michelle. I appreciate it. Although I am sure that Raphael and I have not gone as far as you and Guillaume yet. Like we kiss and hug a bit, but that's it." At this point Stephanie is not sure if she should be disappointed or not. She has to admit that sometimes she imagines being more intimate with Raphael. Or even maybe sleeping on the same bed when they shared the room in Dubai. But he never initiates anything, and she doesn't want to be pushy.

Gaby looks at her sympathetically. "Ah, that's what I thought, too. Steph, Raphael may appear flirty, but when it comes to physical intimacy, I think he prefers to take it slow. This is how we were raised in the family," Gaby says.

Stephanie nods. That may explain why he hasn't made any further move other than kissing.

"I thought it may be because I am a tomboy, and he is not that attracted to me physically, you know." Stephanie starts to feel comfortable opening up about her insecurity to Gaby and Michelle.

Michelle shakes her head. "I am one hundred percent sure that's not the case. I see the way he looked at you when you played the violin in that dress. He is definitely smitten by you."

"Yeah, but that's not my usual self, right? Day-to-day, I always wear something comfortable like jeans and shirts, or workout clothes. And I don't know if I want to change my appearance for the sake of pleasing him. That means I don't have my own personality."

"That's fair. If he really likes you, which I think he does, then he wouldn't mind that you usually wear these types of clothes," Gaby says.

Michelle jumps in, "But on certain occasions, like when you performed with André, you can put in a bit more effort, like you did, by appearing more feminine. Not necessarily to seduce him. It's more to surprise yourself that you can look stunning, too. Tell me, how did you feel when you dressed up and put that makeup on?" Michelle asks.

"Umm.. I felt pretty. Although, I wouldn't do that every day."

"Exactly. You feel pretty, you feel good about yourself. That vibe is what will attract him. Not solely because of the dress or makeup itself," Michelle says.

"Thanks a lot for your advice, Michelle. When it comes to the art of being a woman, I am like a teenager who lacks experience. I haven't really had female friends throughout my life, because I am a tomboy and more sporty than other girls."

"Now you have female friends. Us," Gaby says with a smile.

@@@

Raphael, André, and Guillaume are looking at the king-size bed in front of them without enthusiasm.

"So, how are we going to do this?" André's voice is full of uncertainty. Raphael knows that André probably never really shares bed with guys. Personally, Raphael himself doesn't mind and doesn't care. He went camping a lot, where he had to share a tent with other guys, to sleep in a sleeping bag, and there wasn't that much space from one another. This king-size bed is definitely more comfortable.

"Umm... we will keep our clothes on, I guess," Guillaume says.

"Not a problem for me. I always sleep with clothes on," Raphael says.

"Me, too. But I know André doesn't," Guillaume says.

"Only when I am by myself, or with Gaby," André says.

"Eww. Don't mention that in front of me, please," Raphael says. Raphael always tells his best friends about his love life, which was almost non-existent before he met Stephanie. But André and Guillaume don't really share that much about their love lives because they are dating his sisters. And Raphael prefers not to hear about the private details of their relationships, unless it is something serious that threatens the continuation of the relationship.

After that, they are debating who is going to sleep in the middle. Guillaume finally volunteers. But then, after five minutes trying to sleep, Guillaume gives up and walks out to sleep on the couch in the living room

Raphael's imagination starts running wild. He imagines himself sleeping with Stephanie in this comfortable king-size bed. They cuddle, kiss, and caress each other's body. As much as he wants to go all in, he prefers to take it slow. He would ask her to be his girlfriend first. He wants them to build their relationship based on emotional connection and not just physical connection. For a man, this requires a lot of self-control. But now in his thirties, he knows that he is looking for a wife, and not just a fling like he was in the past.

Regardless, the image of Stephanie in that blue dress, or in her tank tops and shorts when she is working out, or in her swimsuit, he cannot deny the strong attraction and arousal.

He is dreaming of slipping his hand inside her clothes and exploring her muscular body while inhaling her sweet scent. Wait, there is something wrong. Her chest is too flat and muscular to be a woman's breast.

Then he feels that Stephanie is pushing him away. Why?

"Raphael, stop!" He hears André's panicked voice. His eyes snap open.

Instead of finding Stephanie besides him, he finds André in a sitting position on the bed and looking at him in disbelief. Then, André seems very shocked and tries to get off the bed as soon as possible. He rolls from the bed but then falls hard onto the floor.

"Arrrgh."

Now Raphael is fully awake. He tries to find the lamp switch beside the table.

Once he can see the room clearly, he finds André on the floor.

"What's going on?"

Suddenly the door opens. Guillaume seems to hear the commotion from outside.

"Is everything okay?" His eyes are back and forth between Raphael on the bed and André on the floor.

"No, Raphael has just tried to hug me from behind and slipped his hand inside my t-shirt! I'm glad that at least I am wearing a t-shirt." Then André says something in French to Guillaume that sounds like swearing.

Raphael starts to panic. Did he? He has had a naughty dream of Stephanie, could he possibly act on his dream towards André?

Just the thought of it made him sick. His desire for Stephanie must have been very intense then.

"Look, I'm sorry. I was dreaming of ... a girl, but not you, André. I swear. I didn't realize." Raphael doesn't know how to explain his stupidity.

Then Guillaume starts to laugh so hard until he is rolling on the floor.

"Oh my God, Raphael. You are sooo pathetic!" Guillaume continues laughing.

"It's not funny, Guillaume!" André snaps.

"Ha ha, it's extremely funny, André, c'mon. Wait until Gaby and Michelle hear about this." Guillaume is still on the floor laughing and clutching his stomach.

"No way! Then they are going to tell Stephanie. Guillaume, don't do that please." Raphael starts to panic now. He gets off the bed and throws a pillow at Guillaume, "Promise not to tell anyone?"

André slowly recovers from his shock. "Raphael, just to confirm, you are not gay, right? Tell us the truth. Even if you are, I don't care, as long as I am not your target." André asks. His voice still sounds worried.

"Of course not! Even if I was, do you think I will pursue my sister's fiancé, for Christ's sake?"

André seems to be satisfied with this explanation.

"Raphael, you really need to act on your inner desire, man," Guillaume says under the pillow.

Chapter 18

Jerusalem – Dead Sea – Nazareth
Israel, Day 2

Instead of going straight to Nazareth, Raphael and Stephanie decided to go sightseeing in Jerusalem first, and after that Stephanie proposed to go to the Dead Sea before continuing their journey to Nazareth.

"What do you think? Do you feel comfortable visiting the Dead Sea? You don't need to swim if you don't want to. But if you decide to swim, it will be good because you will be floating without doing anything. I think this can be good and safe exposure therapy for you," Stephanie said when they had breakfast in the morning.

Raphael thought for a second before replying, "Sure, why not? I will swim." Stephanie looked very enthusiastic after that.

Then, they said goodbye to André, Guillaume, Gaby, and Michelle. They won't see each other for the next five days.

"It's time to make your dream become reality, Raphael," André said before Raphael left. Raphael's face turned red but he said nothing.

Now Raphael and Stephanie are on the bus to Jerusalem.

"What did André mean about the dream becoming reality?" Stephanie asks.

"Ah, it's nothing... It's just that I have always wanted to go on a multi-day hike like this," Raphael lies. Luckily, Stephanie is not suspicious.

"I see. And did you sleep well last night? No more nightmares?"

'It was a good dream before it turned into a nightmare because of André', Raphael thinks. Why can't he dream about

Stephanie when he is with Stephanie and dream about getting drowned in the swimming pool when he is with André?

"Not last night. Maybe it was because of your music therapy." He smiles at her. "How about you? How's your girls' night with Gaby and Michelle?"

"It was so much fun! They gave me a lot of girly tips, which are what I need." Stephanie laughs enthusiastically. Her laugh and her smiles make Raphael's heart flutter. She seems to have had so much more fun with Gaby and Michelle than he did with André and Guillaume last night.

"Hmm... Glad to hear! But don't change yourself just because of what other girls do. You are beautiful the way you are. And I am not flirting, by the way. I am genuine."

Stephanie pauses for a second before saying, "Thanks, Raphael."

It only takes about one hour to get from Tel Aviv to Jerusalem. By the time they arrive in Jerusalem, it is nine in the morning.

Together Raphael and Stephanie explore the Old City of Jerusalem. Raphael likes the vibe of Jerusalem right away. It's full of buildings made of limestones as well as narrow alleys with steps. It feels ancient, historic, and exotic. The first place they visit is the Wailing Wall, where Jewish people pray. The praying areas for men and women are separated, so Raphael goes to the prayer section on the right and Stephanie goes to the left. In front of the wall, Raphael doesn't know what to pray for. He feels like his life is so good now. So, he gives thanks to God that he has a job that he enjoys, family and friends, and hopefully a girlfriend soon. He also prays for world peace, particularly so that everybody can live together in harmony despite their races, religions, cultures, and languages.

After the Wailing Wall, Raphael reunites with Stephanie and they continue walking around the Old City. They also stop at the Church of the Holy Sepulchre, which is the site where Christians believe that Jesus was crucified. The church is one of the holiest sites for Christians. Raphael also feels grateful to be here. In this church, he prays to become a better person, a better son for his parents, a better brother for his younger sisters, a better friend for André and Guillaume, a better doctor for his patients, as well as a better man for Stephanie.

Raphael then takes the initiative to hold Stephanie's hand. He is happy when she squeezes his hand back. Also, this time he is glad that there is no Brad or Lindsay like when they were in North Korea, so he can have Stephanie all for himself. As Stephanie has been here before, she becomes his tour guide. Every explanation that comes from her mouth is very interesting to him. Unlike when it was Nambok, now Raphael remembers every single thing that she says.

Their next stop is the Arabic market where they have early lunch together. Raphael eats falafel and Stephanie eats kebab. They also share fruits for desserts. Raphael likes this kind of date where they are in a traditional place instead of luxurious places. Stephanie also seems to enjoy exploring the market. Apparently, she likes to cook. Raphael cannot wait to try her cooking.

"Do you want to see a nice view of Jerusalem?" Stephanie asks.

"Yes, I'd love to. Take me there, please." Raphael is excited.

After walking for about thirty minutes, they are standing on the mountain ridge called Mount of Olives. The view from where they stand is incredible. The Old City of Jerusalem is stretched out in front of them. They can see the Dome of the Rock, Al-Aqsa Mosque, as well as the Wailing Wall where they have just been a couple hours ago.

"Wow, Steph. Thanks for bringing me here."

"I knew you would like it."

They admire the view for a few minutes.

"Did you visit Israel by yourself before?" Raphael asks.

"Yes. How did you know?"

"Just guessing. You know, from now on, you don't need to travel by yourself anymore. I will be with you. I want to be with you."

Stephanie doesn't reply. She looks at his eyes deeply and loses her words.

"I love you, Steph."

@@@

I love you, Steph.

On the way from Jerusalem to the Dead Sea, Stephanie cannot stop thinking about what Raphael said. He loves her! She wants to say that she loves him too, but unfortunately, she just froze and was shy after he said it. She looked at the ground and has avoided his eye gaze since then. How stupid she is. 'Say it now', she says to herself. But regardless how many guy friends she has and how tomboyish her appearance is, she is still a girl after all. Now she is waiting for the right moment to say it back to him.

There is no doubt that she loves Raphael. He is a very kind and caring man. He has all the qualities that she values for a life partner. Maybe they didn't grow up in the same culture, but she feels like he is different from other guys from her culture. He is more of a family man and he is not shy to show it. He also treats her like a true gentleman. She knows that many women like to be independent and they don't need gentlemanliness. But again, despite her tomboy appearance, it makes her heart flutter when a guy gives her special treatments. Raphael is definitely that guy who always gives extra care and attention.

They arrive at Kalia Beach at around one-thirty p.m. The view of the Dead Sea is incredible. They can see Jordan from the opposite side. Although it is December, they still can swim thanks to the Mediterranean climate.

Stephanie goes to the women's changing room while Raphael goes to the men's. Stephanie has no choice but to wear her athletic swimsuit again, although it's not ideal in Dead Sea, as she won't swim like in the swimming pool. Her initial plan was only visiting North Korea and not Dubai nor Israel. Looking back, she also didn't expect that Raphael's presence in her vacation would have had this huge impact on her. She smiles to herself.

When she walks back to the shore, Raphael is already there.

"Ready?" Stephanie approaches him.

"Let's go."

They walk towards the water and right away they can feel the salty water sting their skin, especially if they have an open wound. Nevertheless, it is really fun to just float without having to swim. They float on their back while enjoying the view of the sky and the water. It is very relaxing.

"How do you feel being here, does this trigger your trauma?" Stephanie asks.

"Surprisingly not! I feel great. I don't feel like I am going to drown or anything. This is definitely good exposure therapy."

"That's great!"

Then Stephanie realizes how hot Raphael is, especially when he is only wearing his swim trunks. Last time when she saw him change, she didn't pay attention, because he was very sick at that time. But now, she can't help but admire his body. For an Asian man, he is very muscular. Much more muscular than those K-pop idols. His abs are not a six-pack like André's, but are still very firm and toned.

She doesn't understand why a lot of western girls like her don't find Asian men attractive. She personally likes his warm skin color, his small eyes that make him look very smart, his black and straight hair, and the fact that he has less facial and body hair than western men makes him appear more "refined" in her opinion.

She quickly shakes her head, embarrassed at her own thoughts.

"Are you okay?" Raphael asks.

"Yes."

For the next hour, they have fun together and laugh a lot. They also apply mud on each other's body because Dead Sea mud is good for the skin. Again, when Stephanie is applying the mud on Raphael's back, she feels how strong his back is.

At around three p.m., they head back to the changing rooms to shower. After they get dressed, they stand in front of the Dead Sea one last time to admire the beautiful view.

"I will go back here again for sure. This is the only place where I can be surrounded by water and I don't have to be afraid of drowning." Raphael says.

"Yes. And when you are with me, you don't have to be afraid of drowning. I will always watch out for you."

"Thanks, Steph. But may I know why you are doing this for me? Like last time you jumped into the swimming pool with André to save me. Then you took care of me after I had that nightmare."

"Because..." Stephanie looks at the ground. "It's not only you who loves me...I also love you." She is very shy to look into his eyes when saying it.

"I need you to look at me when you say it, because it's the best thing I have heard today." Raphael says in a very gentle voice and he slowly lifts her chin. Now she is looking at his eyes. His face is full of happiness. Stephanie takes a deep breath and gathers her courage.

"I love you, Raphael. And I want to take care of you, too."

This time she says it with conviction.

@@@

They arrive in Nazareth at around seven p.m., which is perfect. They don't want to arrive too late, as they will start their long hike tomorrow.

They check in at Fauzi Azar Inn, which is an ancient Arab mansion, and settle in a mixed-dorm, which is a room with three bunk beds. They will be sharing room with other travelers. There is another couple already occupying a bunk bed in the corner. They quickly introduce themselves and have a small chat.

Although there are private rooms in the inn, Raphael and Stephanie booked the dorm instead. The first reason is because the experience will feel more authentic. Second is because it is cheaper. Another thing that Raphael likes about Stephanie is that she is very down-to-earth and doesn't care that much about luxury. Although, as his feelings towards her get stronger and stronger, he is waiting for the moment that he can share a bed with Stephanie. He regretted that in Dubai, he didn't take this opportunity. And tonight, they will sleep in the bunk bed with Stephanie at the top and him at the bottom. But he reminds himself to be patient. He is sure that there will be plenty of opportunities for the rest of their trip and when they return to Toronto. Also, his style is more taking it slow instead of following the teenagers' hormones and being blinded with lust.

After settling in, they take a tour around the inn, which actually is a very nice place. There is a high-ceilinged lounge with arched windows, as well as a courtyard, kitchen, and dining area. There is also a rooftop which offers a beautiful view of Lower Galilee. At night, Raphael can see Nazareth's night lights. During the day, it must offer the beautiful hill and valley views with antique limestone buildings.

"I really like the accommodation that you chose, Steph. It's very peaceful from over here."

"Yes, I always liked this place," Stephanie says while admiring the view.

Ah, so she must have stayed here during her last visit. However, Raphael cannot imagine how lonely it is to travel and hike by herself. That's how he felt when he hiked the Rocky Mountains in Alberta by himself. He hopes that she will never be alone again.

After that, they chill in the lounge while chatting with the other travelers again. Raphael notices how Stephanie is able to mingle with all kinds of people from different backgrounds. First with Gaby, Michelle, and him who are Asian-Canadians; second with André and Guillaume who are from Quebec; then with some European and Australian tourists they met in North Korea. And now with other European travelers as well as with local Muslims, Jewish people, and Christians.

It requires an open mind as well as a deep level of empathy to be able to adapt like she does. Also, her profession as music therapist must help one way or another. The more Raphael spends time with Stephanie, the more he falls in love with her.

Chapter 19

Nazareth – Cana
Israel, Day 3

After breakfast the next day, Raphael and Stephanie begin their journey. They start from the center of Nazareth at the Basilica of Annunciation, which is a church built to commemorate when Angel Gabriel gave good news to Mother Mary that she would give birth to Jesus.

After that, they pass through the old city of Nazareth before going up the stairs that lead them to the ridge. This time, they can see Nazareth and the Galilean landscape during the daytime from the ridge. Stephanie looks at Raphael who is beside her. He looks like he is really enjoying the view as much as she is. She feels satisfied. Although she has done this hike before, she realizes that it is so much more fulfilling to share it with someone. Especially when you see that person's face is full of happiness.

Then, they continue their long walk to the north. As an experienced hiker, Stephanie has prepared for this long walk. She packed really light and she left some stuff in Tel Aviv, including her violin. She wears good boots and she brings sufficient water and snacks as well as some band aids in case of blisters. Raphael also carries pretty much the same things, plus some more first aid and medical kits. He also has to leave some of his medical kits in Tel Aviv, and brings only the essentials.

At some point, they pass Tzipori National Park, which is an archeological site that shows the remnants of Roman, Jewish, Byzantine, and Ottoman's cultures. For example, there is a Roman theater, villa, and ancient reservoir; a Jewish Quarter; a Crusade Castle; and a Synagogue. In some buildings, there are beautiful mosaic floors that illustrate symbols and stories. It feels like they are transported back to ancient times. They could spend the whole day in this place, but unfortunately, they have to continue on to reach Cana before it gets dark.

After that, they pass a pine forest which also offers a natural and calming view. Stephanie always likes this type of outdoor activity where they are all surrounded by the green nature.

"I always thought nothing can beat the hikes in the Rocky Mountains. But I am surprised how this type of hike can be very rewarding, too. It offers various landscapes like villages, hills, valleys, and forests," Raphael says.

"I know right. Also, I think it's not very demanding physically. Like we don't have to scramble or anything. There will be some steep sections later on when we get to the mountain, but it's manageable."

Then Raphael and Stephanie talk about their hiking experiences in the Rockies. She enjoys climbing difficult mountains in Alberta and apparently Raphael is the same! They compare the mountains that they both have climbed; the mountains that one has climbed and the other hasn't; as well as the mountains that neither of them has climbed.

Raphael appears very enthusiastic when talking about hikes. "So, do you want to go to Lake Louise next summer and climb Devil's Thumb? I heard it's not that difficult. Honestly, I am thirty years old now, I feel pretty old to climb difficult mountains."

Stephanie laughs. He must be joking. Raphael doesn't seem old at all. She feels like he is still in his prime years by looking at how he works out in the gym as well as his muscular body. And she likes it that he has made a plan together for next summer. That means she is not just a vacation fling.

"Sure! I am in," She is excited.

After that they head towards the east and pass Mashhad, an Arab village that has a population around eight thousand people, before entering Cana. Once they arrive at Cana, they visit the Fransiscan Wedding Church. It is believed that this is where Jesus performed his first miracle, which was turning water into wine at a wedding. Many couples renew their wedding vows here.

@@@

Raphael likes the church right away. From the outside, it looks like a house. But when they enter the inside, it's actually a Basilica. The inside is very peaceful and it feels like home. This makes him long to share a home with someone. Raphael looks at Stephanie from the corner of his eyes. As much as he wants this woman to be that person, they have only known each other for about a month and a half. He hopes to get to know her a bit more.

"My mom should visit here with my dad someday. They will like it," Raphael comments when they sit inside the church.

"My parents have been here. They love it! Even for my mom, who is not a Christian."

"Oh, what's your mom's religion?"

"She is Jewish."

Raphael is intrigued right away. "Wow, so you are half-Jewish. I didn't know that." So, this may explain why she looks very comfortable in Israel.

"Yes. I can actually obtain an Israeli passport under the Law of Return."

"Are you going to?" Raphael hopes that she doesn't have any plan to leave Canada.

"Maybe someday. Right now, I haven't seen any reason why I have to. But Canada will always be my home." Raphael is relieved after she says that.

"Do you speak Hebrew or practice Judaism?"

"I can read biblical Hebrew texts and recite some prayers. I only go to Synagogue during Yom Kippur or Rosh Hashanah every year. But that's it. I cannot speak or write modern Hebrew. Maybe I can understand a little bit when someone speaks Hebrew."

"That's impressive!"

"Thanks."

"And so... umm... if you don't mind me asking, as a half-Jewish and half-Christian, do you believe in Jesus?"

Stephanie laughs. Raphael hopes that he is not very blunt with his question. But Stephanie appears to enjoy the conversation that they have instead of getting offended.

"Hmm... my parents always avoid this conversation, actually. But for me personally, how do I put this... I believe in love. When God delivered the Israelites from Egypt through Moses, He did it because He loved His people. When God saves us through Jesus' sacrifice on the cross, it's because He loves us. I don't care if Moses or Jesus really did what they did or not. But I look at their fruits or their influence in the world, and if the fruits are faith, hope, and love, then yes, I believe it."

Raphael is speechless for a while. He really likes her open-mindedness. She focuses on the similarities instead of the differences, like most people who cause war. If many people can think like her, there will be less or no war.

"How about Islam?"

"It's the same thing. If Prophet Muhammad taught about love, forgiveness, faith, justice, et cetera, then this teaching bears good fruits. I believe that all religions are basically trying to explain the same thing, but from different perspectives. It's like the blind men and the elephant. When you ask each blind man to describe the elephant based on what they touch, some may describe the side; some may describe the face or the tail. But at the end everybody tries to explain the same elephant. It's the same thing with religions. Some religions may reveal more than the others, but at the end, we try to describe faith, hope, and love."

Raphael is again speechless by her point of view. He never thought of religions in that sense! For him, he just follows what his parents and his teacher taught him. He never dares to question it or even consider other religions.

"How about you, Raphael? Do you believe in God, especially as a doctor?" Stephanie asks.

"Yes, I believe in the existence of 'God' or 'Creator'. It's because the way the human body works, you know, how the mechanism is so perfect and everything is automated. For example, our immune system, reproductive, cardiovascular, digestive system, and so on. So, this must point out to a very intelligent creator, whom I believe to be God. And when I look at the beautiful nature during hikes or travel, I cannot imagine how something that beautiful can exist on its own without a beautiful and thoughtful creator? And when humans are naturally longing for love for one another, whether it's in a family or friends or romantic setting, it's just showing that we are not robots. Every creation must reflect their creators. So, it only makes sense if our Intelligent Creator is also a very Loving Creator."

"But what about some people who did evil stuff? Like they murder each other, they steal, and all this hatred?"

"It's because our Loving Creator loves us too much to the point that He gave us freedom before we were mature and wise enough to decide what's good for us. Look at the newborns or toddlers or children. In their early years, they were very pure and innocent. But once they start seeing the world, their minds get exposed to bad influence and get corrupted. Humans get hurt by other humans and they end up hurting each other. But that's because of the influence of other humans, not necessarily because of the Creator."

"Wow, I also like your point of view."

"Thanks. But again, we never know if our point of view is right or not. We are just blind men trying to describe an elephant." They laugh together after he says that.

He continues, "Nevertheless, despite what religion I believe, I just want to be a better person."

"You are such a good person, Raphael. I have never met anyone like you before." Stephanie blushes a little bit when she says that.

He looks her in the eyes and holds her hand.

"You too, Steph. The more I know you, the more I love you."

He gently kisses her forehead.

@@@

Tonight, they settle in Cana Palace. The accommodation feels like a minimalist apartment instead of a hotel. But they like it. This time they booked a one-bedroom.

Today they have walked about fifteen kilometers. Now that she has showered and is lying on the bed, she feels tired. Raphael is currently showering in the bathroom. She is a bit nervous now. Tonight is the second time they are going to sleep in the same bed. The first time was in North Korea, but that didn't count because they were just comforting each other. What will happen tonight? They have been connected emotionally and spiritually for the past few weeks. Will tonight be the moment when they connect physically? Despite the religious teaching that she embraces, she feels like if she is sure that she loves Raphael wholeheartedly, she is ready to give all of herself to him. They are not even boyfriend and girlfriend yet! But if they love each other deeply, does relationship status matter? At least in her culture, no. She knows some people have sex first to determine if they are sexually compatible or not before committing to each other. But she remembers that Gaby said that Raphael grew up differently and he prefers to take things slow.

Raphael comes out from the shower, fully dressed in his t-shirt and shorts with a towel hanging around his neck. Stephanie is a bit disappointed.

"Are you okay, Steph?" Raphael dries his hair with the towel.

"Yes, I am. Why do you ask?"

"I don't know. You look...tired."

"I am okay. We still have three more days for the hike. Let's go to sleep," Stephanie says, and turns off the lights so that he cannot see her face. She feels a mix of nervousness and disappointment.

"Good idea," Raphael says, and gets under the blanket with her. She feels his leg brushes against hers. And when she smells his aftershave and his masculine scent, she feels like her heart starts slamming her chest. Her hormones surge.

They are lying down next to each other without sound for a while. Stephanie is fully awake; and she is pretty sure Raphael is not asleep either, as sometimes he sighs and then switches sides.

"Steph?"

"Yes?"

"Umm... nothing."

Then, it is silent again.

And finally, Raphael takes the initiative first.

He slowly turns his body towards her. She also turns her body towards him. Then they start kissing each other. He starts with caressing her face, then her shoulder, and then he slips his hand under her t-shirt while they are still kissing. His hand is very skillful. First, he places it against her belly and then moves up to her chest, her back, and finally he unhooks her bra.

She also pulls his shirt over his head and she explores his body. They are slowly undressing each other until they are only in their underwear. She likes feeling his skin against hers.

When she tries to pull down his underwear, he stops her.

"Steph."

"Yes?"

"I think this is the furthest I can go. I am sorry," Raphael says. As the room is quite dark, she cannot see his face clearly. She cannot guess what he is thinking. He doesn't want her, is that it?

"What do you mean?"

Raphael sighs before answering. "I don't want to start using you for my pleasure. I want to make love with you, but right now I am kind of mixing my love with pleasure, which I don't think is healthy for our relationship."

"I don't think I understand."

"How about we wait? How about we return to Toronto, continue our relationship in reality, not just in an adventurous and romantic setting like this, and then we commit to each other and I can give all myself to you."

"You mean, you think we are doing this right now because we got carried away in this adventure? Not because we really love each other?"

"No, I am sure that I love you and I want to make love with you. But if we start doing that, I am afraid that the pleasure will distract me from loving you wholeheartedly."

"So, when do you think we are able to separate love from pleasure? People can love each other and please each other at the same time, right? Isn't the pleasure the bonus that comes from loving someone?"

"I will be able to separate love from pleasure when I have seen the worst of you and I still love you, and I still imagine my future with you. I really treasure you, Stephanie. I don't want to have sex with you and then it turns out that we are not meant to be together. That would be unfair for you."

She feels like someone stabbed her chest. So, he doubts that they have a future together. It's not that she herself is currently sure that Raphael is the one for her. But at this point she really loves him and she is ready to give all herself to him.

"Are you by any chance not attracted to me, physically? Because I am too muscular and tomboyish?" Doubt starts to creep in her head.

"I am very attracted to you, Steph," Raphael says. Then he gets off the bed and turns on the light.

Even when he is standing there half-naked in his boxers only, she still can see that he is very aroused. Wow. She wants to be united with him so badly.

Raphael turns off the light and slips under the blanket beside her again. He puts his arm around her and places her head on his chest.

"Believe me when I say I love you, Steph. You are too precious for me. If I was only looking for a hookup, we would already have had sex by now. But you are definitely something more special."

"I see. That's okay. I respect your decision," she says. She puts her arm around his waist.

"Thank you. And again, you cannot imagine how hard it is for me. You are always in my head. I always imagine and fantasize about you. But that's pleasure. I want to be certain first that I will love you in any circumstances before benefiting from the pleasure that I can get from you."

In the beginning, she thought Raphael had a more western mindset as she has as he grew up in Canada. And he used to be so flirty before. Apparently, Raphael is much more conservative than he appears. She is not sure how she feels about that. Maybe this is the first time they encounter a cultural barrier. It will take her sometimes to understand his perspective. But isn't it what love is? Understanding, respect, and patience?

Although she feels rejected in a way, she appreciates that Raphael tries his best not to hurt her feelings.

She decides to let this slide and tries to sleep.

At least they cuddle for the entire night.

Chapter 20

Cana – Kibbutz Lavi
Israel, Day 4

Stephanie tries to forget what happened last night. They haven't talked much since they started the hike today. Raphael seems to be busy in his own thoughts.

Since last night, she has been thinking about what Raphael said. She knows that he meant well. He really cared about her and he actually behaved like a true gentleman. He is not one of those guys who just use women during the night, and disappear in the morning. And she agreed that they haven't known each other that long, and there is no guarantee of their future together at this point. Raphael has made it clear, until there is commitment and a future together, there will be no sex. And he did it for her own good. Then why hasn't he asked her to be his girlfriend?

As someone who is also logical, Stephanie knows that he may want to wait until they finish their trip. They will see if their lifestyle is compatible with each other under their regular routine. She knows that he sometimes has night shifts, so they may not be able to spend twenty-four hours straight together like now. They also haven't known each other's annoying or bad habits that could be a deal breaker.

Therefore, from a logical standpoint, she understands Raphael's reasoning, and she admits that it makes so much sense. But how about from an emotional standpoint? If she is just following her emotions, she is currently head over heels for him. If he asked her to be his girlfriend right now, she would say yes. But is it wise? Probably not. This is real life, not a fairy tale. They need to come back to their real life in Toronto first before deciding.

Stephanie is a little bit embarrassed as she almost got carried away with her emotions. She felt disappointed that Raphael didn't move forward further last night. But now that she thinks about it, he is right. She is impressed by Raphael's integrity and self-control. Although he may appear impulsive and blunt sometimes, he is actually very cool-headed, and he calculates every risk. This shows maturity that she values in a partner.

After she rationalizes what happened, she feels better. Now she can focus on enjoying the hike. Currently, they are on the ridge where they can see the beautiful Tur'an valley and Tur'an town stretched out below. After that, they pass through Beit Keshet Forest which has a lot of expansive green scenery. There is also an army base in the forest. Today, the walk is approximately fourteen kilometres, which is slightly shorter than yesterday. However, she can feel that she is gradually getting more tired than usual. Maybe because she didn't get enough sleep yesterday, thinking about Raphael all night.

"Steph, don't forget to drink your water, and don't hesitate to take a break if you feel tired," Raphael says from behind her.

"Oh, yes, that's true. Thanks for reminding me." She drinks her water.

Raphael stops in front of her. "Are you still thinking about yesterday?" he asks carefully.

"I was a few minutes ago, but now I feel good about it. You are right. We shouldn't rush things. And I appreciate that you are thinking about what's best for me, instead of just what you want."

Raphael looks relieved after she said that. "I am glad that you understand. And believe me when I say I am smitten by you."

She laughs. "Okay, I believe you."

They continue their walk. Stephanie is glad that there is no more awkwardness between them. But even though she feels like her mind is lighter, she feels like her body is getting heavier. She also feels dizzy and lightheaded. Maybe she overestimates her own stamina.

They are walking on the ancient road near Golani Junction when Stephanie suddenly trips and falls forward into the dirt road.

"Steph!" Raphael sounds panicked and he quickly helps her get up. "Are you okay?"

"Yes, I think I am. Uh, this is embarrassing." She notices that her knees start to bleed, as well as her right palm.

"Let's sit so that I can have a look." He leads her to the green grass.

He examines her wounds carefully. Then he opens his backpack and takes out his medical supplies. He starts washing her knees and palm with water and then applies antiseptics. After that he wraps both her injured knees and her right hand with gauze and tapes. He does it all very quickly and efficiently.

"Thanks, Raphael," she says after he finishes.

"No problem." He puts all his medical supplies back into his bag.

She is about to continue walking but Raphael grabs her arm.

"Wait, let's sit down for a while. Tell me honestly, how are you feeling?"

She feels like she cannot hide anything from him.

"A bit tired, to be honest. I don't know why, we haven't walked that far today. I am usually not this weak."

"You are not weak, Steph. Are you still on your period?" Raphael asks. Seriously, do they have to discuss this now?

"No, it finished a couple of days ago."

"Okay. I feel like you are overexerting yourself. You are traveling across three countries for the past two weeks plus working out, swimming, skydiving, and now hiking."

"I think you are right."

"Let's take a break. Here, drink more water and eat some snacks." Raphael gives his water bottle and snacks to her. She follows his instructions.

They sit for a while and enjoy the green scenery. It feels quiet and they don't see other travelers. Because she is tired, she leans her head on Raphael's shoulder. She feels grateful that she is not alone.

Raphael puts his arm around her shoulder. "I am worried about you, Steph. We are not even halfway to Capernaum. We still have two more days, and the next two days will be longer than today and yesterday, right?"

"Yes. But don't worry. I know my body well. Tonight, I will sleep earlier. And tomorrow I will be energized again."

"Okay." He caresses her head gently.

After resting for twenty minutes, she proposes to continue their journey. Raphael quickly checks her pulse before nodding. "We can continue at a slower pace. And give your backpack to me."

"What? No way." Is he crazy? He wants to carry her backpack on top of his own? There is no way she is going to let him do that.

"Steph, do you trust me?"

"No."

"Let me carry your backpack at least until we see the Kibbutz." The Kibbutz is not too far from here. It's probably about three kilometres.

Stephanie is thinking. He doesn't have to do that. She still has the energy to carry her backpack on her own. She can force herself. But his tone is very commanding and undebatable.

She has no other choice than giving her backpack to him. "I am sorry to be a burden."

"You are not a burden at all. We are a team. When you are down, I will lift you up. And vice-versa." He carries her backpack on his front and his own backpack on his back.

"Also, let's walk at a slow but steady pace. Take a deep breath through your nose and exhale through your mouth. And don't wait until you feel thirsty to drink water. Can you do that for me?"

"Yes."

"Okay, let's go."

They continue walking along the Roman Road, a paved road built by the Roman Empire. At that time, paved roads were a privilege. It is also easier for her to walk on.

Without her backpack, she feels better and lighter. Although she is limping, she feels better than before, thanks to Raphael's reminders for a slow and steady pace, deep breathing, and drinking water. It's not that she doesn't know all of this. But sometimes she is too excited, gets carried away, and forgets about these things.

@@@

Raphael is busy watching over Stephanie for the next hour. Earlier she looked pale and out of breath. Now at least she looks better. But seeing her limping makes him want to protect her even more.

His shoulder and back are hurting from carrying two backpacks but he doesn't care. He is also almost running out of water because he used his water to wash Stephanie's wounds earlier. Now he has to carefully ration his water until they reach Kibbutz Lavi. His throat starts to feel dry. But at this point, Stephanie needs to be prioritized before him.

By the time they reach Kibbutz Lavi, they both are very tired and thirsty. They feel so relieved when they can finally check into the hotel, drink plenty of water, and eat a fancy kosher dinner. The amenities in Kibbutz Lavi hotel are very nice. There is a swimming pool, a gym, various courts, as well as jogging and biking trails. But since they have done enough exercise for the day, they decide to just rest instead of enjoying these facilities. Stephanie also agrees and doesn't complain. With her injured knees, she cannot do sports as usual. At least they can enjoy the breathtaking view of the Galilean mountains from this luxurious hotel and rest comfortably tonight.

Once they get to their room, Raphael checks on Stephanie's knees and palm again to make sure that her wounds are not infected. After that, they take turns to shower and go to bed right away. He hugs Stephanie from behind all night and prays that she doesn't get sick.

Chapter 21

Kibbutz Lavi – Moshav Arbel
Israel, Day 5

The next day doesn't look promising. They wake up late and the sky outside of the window is gray. It looks like it's going to rain soon.

While Stephanie seems to have more energy than yesterday, it's Raphael's turn to feel unwell. His throat hurts since last night and he starts to feel a slight headache. Maybe he is also overestimating his stamina.

"It looks like it's gonna rain. Are you okay with this?" Raphael asks.

"Yes. I am okay. How about you?"

"I am okay, too."

Then, they continue their third day of hike. Today the distance is about seventeen kilometres, which is longer than yesterday. The terrain is also more difficult. Half an hour after they start walking, the thunderstorm begins. They start to soak in the rain.

"Oh, no. Now your wounds are all wet. It must hurt." Raphael notices Stephanie's knees and palms.

"It stings a bit, but it's okay. I can manage. Don't worry about me." Stephanie looks at him with a smile. They both are wet and cold. But to his eyes, Stephanie looks very pretty with her wet hair and wet face. He admires her for a second, not only her looks, but also her resilience to continue with their hike.

"Are you sure you are okay yourself? Your voice sounds a bit hoarse," Stephanie asks.

"I have a sore throat, but it's okay."

"It's not okay when it's raining and cold like this. Hang on." Then she takes out a scarf from her backpack and puts it around his neck.

"Thanks, Steph. Now your scarf is wet, though."

"Don't worry about it."

They continue walking past the Horns of Hattin, where Saladin defeated the Crusaders in 1187. After that, they ascend a staircase and arrive at a hilltop that offers another gorgeous view. They start to be able to see the Sea of Galilee. Even in the middle of heavy rain, they still see the villages and highways, as well as the expansive fields below.

The next few hours become more challenging. Now they have to walk through the boulders that are slippery, especially in the rain. Raphael makes sure he walks close to Stephanie so that he can catch her if she falls. Her knees wounds will be extremely painful if she falls on her knees again, as they haven't fully healed.

Unfortunately, as much as Raphael wants to take care of Stephanie, he can feel that his body is also defeated because of the tiredness, sore throat, headache, and the cold from the rain. He can feel that his temperature is rising. He starts to shiver as well because of the chills.

"I am sorry, I didn't expect that it would rain this heavily," Stephanie says when they are in the middle of going through these boulders carefully.

"Why are you sorry? It's okay. It's fun to be challenged like this. Aren't we adrenaline junkies?" Raphael tries to lighten up the mood.

"But you start to get sick. Do you think I don't notice that your voice is getting very hoarse and you start coughing, too?"

"Don't worry about me. I have a good immune system. I will recover quickly."

Despite his physical condition, he is still glad to have company like Stephanie. She navigates through these boulders skillfully. He knows that she can go much faster, but she is waiting for him. Usually, he can pass these boulders easily, too, but not today. He almost stumbles several times. His physical condition is really slowing him down.

@@@

Tel Aviv

André, Guillaume, Gaby, and Michelle are enjoying their lunches at one of the restaurants along Rothschild Boulevard. Although the lunches are very good, the four of them seem to be uneasy about something.

"Do you think it's raining where they hike?" Guillaume asks while looking at the gray sky above them.

"I think so. It's even a thunderstorm." André checks his phone.

"Do you think they are okay?" Gaby asks worriedly.

"I know they brought a rain jacket. But is it enough? They are walking in the wilderness for hours now. And Raphael hasn't answered my text," Michelle adds.

Gaby sighs. For some reason she can feel whenever her brother is in trouble. Maybe it's a sibling's instinct.

"I think Raphael is in trouble," André suddenly says. Everybody is now looking at him.

"What? How do you know? Don't make me scared, please," Michelle says.

"I don't know if this is superstitious or not, but since Raphael saved my life last year, I feel an inexplicably strong connection with him. Like I can sense it when he is in trouble," André says.

"How is that possible?" Guillaume asks.

"I am not sure. You said at some point I stopped breathing and he gave me rescue breaths before they gave me oxygen?" André asks. Guillaume nods.

"I heard that you will always have this type of connection with your lifesaver," André continues.

Michelle seems doubtful, "What about other people that Raphael has saved in the ER? Do they have this type of connection with Raphael, then?"

Gaby jumps in, "In the ER, I doubt it was him who directly saved patients' lives with his hands. He usually runs the code or gives instructions and it's the nurses and others who personally save them, right? But in André's case, it's Raphael who did it."

André continues, "Like last time, when he was fighting with those guys in Dubai, I could feel that he was in trouble. I feel it again now."

Now everybody looks worried.

"Let's pray for Raphael and Stephanie." Gaby proposes. She grabs André and Michelle's hands, as they are sitting next to her. André and Michelle grab Guillaume's hands.

"I will pray to Buddha," Michelle says.

"I will just follow along, as I am not a believer," Guillaume says.

"I will pray to Jesus," Gaby says.

"I am not a believer but I will pray to Jesus, God, and Allah since we are in the Holy Land," André says. They take a moment of silence and pray according to their own beliefs.

After they are done praying, André adds, "I feel worse. I feel like this is only the beginning of Raphael's problem. It will get worse."

@@@

Moshav Arbel

Stephanie keeps glancing at Raphael worriedly. They still have an hour left. It seems like his condition is getting worse. He took some fever medicine half an hour ago, but his temperature keeps rising to forty degrees Celsius. He looks extremely pale and out of breath. And it is still raining heavily.

Under normal weather, if it was not raining, they could hike this path easily. However, the rain makes it slower for them as they have to be careful not to slip.

"I think we need to stop," Stephanie proposes.

"No, we need to keep going. The longer we stay in this cold weather the more dangerous for us," Raphael says with a weak voice. He puts both of his hands on his knees while panting hard.

"Okay, give me your backpack, then."

"Are you kidding me? No."

"But you helped me yesterday. Now let me help you."

"Maybe we can transfer some of the things in my backpack to yours? But not all. Gosh, I feel so bad."

"Great idea."

They stop for a bit just so that Stephanie can transfer some of Raphael's stuff to her backpack. She takes the water bottle, medical kits, and some clothes.

"Okay. Now it should be lighter." She gives back the backpack to him.

"Thank you, Steph. I really appreciate it."

They continue walking as fast as Raphael can. Stephanie has no idea how he can climb a steep slope in this condition. Compared to him, the wounds on her knees seem trivial. She has abandoned the bandage, as it was all wet because of the rain.

Usually, Raphael is always humorous and chatty. It's a bit alarming to Stephanie when he is quiet like this. He must feel very sick and uncomfortable.

It takes forever before they finally arrive at Arbel Holidays Homes at Moshav Arbel. The accommodation is a nice wooden cabin in the mountain where they can see the Sea of Galilee. She is glad that they booked a room for couples with a jacuzzi.

Right after they settle in their room, Stephanie fills the jacuzzi with warm water. After that they strip off their wet clothes and submerge inside the jacuzzi. Raphael seems like he can pass out at any time. She puts her hand on his forehead. It seems that his fever is slightly better. She grabs his hand under the water.

"After this I am going to order dinner and you will drink a warm beverage and feel better." She tries to comfort him.

"I already feel better thanks to you," Raphael says with his eyes closed.

"Do you still have a sore throat?"

"Yes. But it's better now."

After they finish taking a bath, they get dressed and she orders food. Raphael is also re-dressing her wounds. Even when he himself is not feeling well, he still takes care of her.

They eat the homemade warm soup, bread, salads with olive oil, and chicken with hummus that night. They also drink hot tea with lemon and honey. Although they don't have much appetite, they have to force themselves to eat so that they have enough energy to finish their last day of hiking tomorrow.

Raphael takes more fever medicine before going to bed. He mentions that under normal situations, he wouldn't take any medicine and would let his immune system fight the illness naturally. But for the sake of comfort tonight and tomorrow during the hike, he takes the medicine. He also gargles salt water.

That night Stephanie hugs Raphael from behind to keep him warm.

Chapter 22

Moshav Arbel – Capernaum
Israel, Day 6

Raphael feels better the next day. He regains his energy and is ready for the last and longest day of the hike. He thinks that this is the miracle that happened in Holy Land, which is when his body recovers very quickly. He still feels the tiredness, but no more headache, chills, nor sore throat. Only a very mild cough, but he still can breathe normally.

The support from Stephanie since yesterday really made a difference. If he hiked this trail alone with a condition like yesterday, he thought that he wouldn't make it. He feels like they make such a great team, taking care of each other during difficult situations.

He glances at Stephanie several times when they hike Mount Arbel. The rain from yesterday is delaying the recovery of her knees, but he dressed up her wounds again this morning and hopefully her knees will recover soon. He can see how strong and resilient Stephanie is. Hiking when you injure your knees is not easy at all. Plus, she was taking care of him yesterday.

The view of the Sea of Galilee from Mount Arbel is incredible. For a moment, he forgot how hard it is to get here. He forgot all the obstacles that they have faced to arrive at this point. Now looking at this beautiful view, it feels like it's all worth it.

"Are you feeling better, Raphael?" Stephanie asks while they are enjoying the view.

"Yes! Thanks for taking care of me yesterday."

"No problem. You did the same to me."

Raphael puts his arm around her shoulder. Yesterday, he felt so sick to the point that he didn't even talk that much. Now, he wants to have fun with Stephanie.

"I will never forget this view."

"Me neither. Although I have seen this view, it's better when I enjoy it with you. I really treasure the memory that we have together."

"Me, too. These past two and half weeks have been the best moments in my life, despite being sick yesterday."

"I didn't realize that we have only been on this trip for two and half weeks. I feel like we have traveled together much longer than that. Thanks for accompanying me."

"Thanks for accompanying me, too. I cannot wish for a better company." Although they have only known each other for a couple of months and travelled together for two and half weeks, Raphael feels like they have known each other for such a long time. She is very familiar and comforting. She makes him feel at home. He is grateful to have her.

After that they have to climb down the cliff. Luckily, the weather is nice today. If they have to climb down this cliff in a weather like yesterday, it will be extremely dangerous. They pass the Bedouin Village before arriving at the Galilean coastline. Then, they continue to walk towards the north of the Sea of Galilee for quite some time before arriving at Tabgha, where Jesus fed five thousand people. Finally, they can take a break and enjoy the relaxing and peaceful scenery by the lake. Raphael starts to imagine that he will grow old with Stephanie, and when they retire, they will move here and fish every day.

"Do you still have energy to climb the Mount Beatitudes? It's only a hill, not a real mountain. But don't force yourself if you are tired," Stephanie says.

"Of course not. Let's go." He is excited to explore the area more.

They start ascending Mount Beatitudes, and as Stephanie said, it's a very easy and short hike. Again, they can see the beautiful Sea of Galilee from the top of the hill. He likes that he can enjoy the view of the Sea of Galilee from multiple angles during this hike. He is always amazed by the view regardless how many times he sees it. He understands why Stephanie likes this hike, too.

There is also a church on the mountain called the Church of the Beatitudes. This spot is believed to be where Jesus delivered the Sermon on the Mount. They go inside to admire the Neo-Byzantine architecture, the mosaics, and the octagonal shape that represents the eight Beatitudes. Raphael doesn't remember what the eight Beatitudes are, so he asks Stephanie.

"If I was not mistaken, it's to bless and encourage those who are poor in spirit, meek, mourn, hungry and thirsty after justice, merciful, clean of heart, peacemakers, and suffer persecution for the sake of justice. Basically, it's saying that there is hope in God and in heaven for these people."

"I see. You know a lot, Steph. I am impressed."

"Thank you. I hope you don't mind that our adventure here sometimes turns into something spiritual."

"Of course not. I always want to find meaning in my life. And sometimes getting deeper into our spirituality adds more meaning into our lives, too," he says.

"That's true. Although it may seem unrelated, I find that adventure and spirituality go hand-in-hand. Like we overcome our fear; we get to know ourselves, especially our strengths and weaknesses; we question our purpose in life, et cetera."

"I agree. And I like that I am doing this 'spiritual adventure' with you, Steph. You are the perfect person for this. You inspire a huge reflection in me. Especially about myself and my life."

"So do you."

"Although I enjoy being here with you, I really cannot wait for us to go back to Toronto and continue our relationship, start our lives together..." Raphael stops. Is he imagining too much? What if Stephanie hasn't thought that far? Is he making her overwhelmed with all these expectations? But Stephanie clears his doubt right away.

She looks him in the eyes and says, "Me, too, Raphael. I know that we are very compatible in doing adventures together. But I trust that we are also compatible in real life. I cannot wait to build a life together with you."

@@@

Capernaum - Tel Aviv

It feels rewarding to finally complete the hike. They have an early supper at Capernaum and then visit the Capernaum Synagogue before taking a bus back to Tel Aviv. Raphael is happy that Stephanie can enjoy both church and synagogue visits, which are part of her two identities as Jewish and Christian.

They walk towards Kfar Nahum intersection to catch the bus. Raphael cannot wait until they arrive at Tel Aviv and both he and Stephanie can recuperate properly. Although he feels better than yesterday, he knows that he is still not one hundred percent in good shape. So is Stephanie. This hike is really taking a toll on their health. They will return straight to Toronto from Tel Aviv, for sure.

The bus ride takes more than three hours and they need to transfer multiple times. So, he and Stephanie take turns to sleep on the bus, as they don't want to miss their stops.

Somewhere along the way when they are already pretty close to Tel Aviv, there is a sudden jolt and loud explosion. Raphael feels his body is thrown. He also notices the horror when the bus they are riding turns upside down, but his brain is too shocked to process what he is seeing. He opens his mouth but he cannot scream. He feels his side hit the bus wall very hard. Then everything goes black.

@@@

Tel Aviv

André is in the middle of enjoying his drink while looking at the view of Tel Aviv from his suite window, when he suddenly feels a sharp chest pain.

"Ugh." He clutches his chest automatically.

Guillaume, who is standing nearby, notices what happened right away.

"André, what's going on?" He quickly approaches André and turns his body towards him.

"I... don't know. I felt a sharp chest pain for a second." André puts down his glass and takes a deep breath. He feels that his heart skips a beat.

"Is this related to your heart condition?" Guillaume's voice starts to panic.

"No, I don't think so. It's gone now." Although the pain is only one second, the anxiety persists. André feels uneasy, but he doubts that this has anything to do with his heart condition.

"You made me scared for a second." Guillaume sighs. "I wish Raphael was here. He will be able to tell what's wrong. He is going to arrive soon, right?"

"Yes." When Guillaume mentions Raphael's name, André starts to feel uneasy again. He really hopes he is just imagining things. He decides to sit on the couch, wondering if he should tell Gaby or not.

Meanwhile, Gaby is in the middle of chatting with Michelle in the bedroom when she feels a sudden sharp pain in her stomach.

"Ugh." She clutches her stomach.

"Gabs! Are you okay?" Now Michelle starts to panic.

"Yeah, I think I am. Suddenly my stomach hurt for a second. But now I am feeling okay," Gaby says. Michelle examines Gaby's face closer. She looks pale now.

"It's weird, you are not about to perform piano. Why do you have a stomach pain now?" Michelle knows that Gaby usually has pre-performance anxiety before her piano recital or exam, and the anxiety is usually manifested in the form of stomach pain. Michelle used to feel the same in the beginning of her ballet career, but now she is good at handling it.

"I am not sure," Gaby says. She looks uneasy.

"When is Raphael arriving? He will be able to tell what's wrong," Michelle says.

Hearing Raphael's name gives another sharp pain in her stomach again, although it's not as intense as earlier.

"Michelle, what if something happens to Raphael?" Gaby looks panicked now.

"What do you mean?"

"Let's find André and Guillaume." Gaby gets off the bed and walks towards the door. Michelle follows her.

They find André and Guillaume sitting on the couch, looking as uneasy as them. Gaby and Michelle join them on the couch.

"André..." Gaby starts but she doesn't know how to explain what she feels. It will make her sound paranoid. But Gaby doesn't need to finish her sentence, André can already guess.

"Are you thinking about Raphael?" He moves to sit beside her and grabs her hand. Guillaume also moves to sit beside Michelle.

Gaby nods quietly. André sighs. "Me, too. Do you think something bad happened to him?"

Gaby nods again. She buries her face in André's chest. He hugs her tight.

"I can feel it, too." His voice now sounds alarmed.

Chapter 23

Tel Aviv

Raphael doesn't know how long he passed out. Once he wakes up, he finds himself lying on the street. A lot of people are screaming and crying. He also cannot see clearly as there is a lot of smoke.

Something must have happened. Now that he has become more alert, he can see ambulances and paramedics everywhere. No way. What has happened? He remembers that he was on the bus; why is he now in the street? Did they get into an accident?

He tries to assess himself. He doesn't feel any pain right now. But it could be because his body is full of epinephrine. He tries to breathe and yes, he can breathe. He tries to move his body starting from his fingers and toes. They are all fine. He tries to roll himself on the side and is hoping that he doesn't sustain spinal injury. It doesn't seem so. He gets up and glances over his body. His clothes are covered in dust and turn black. But everything seems okay from the outside.

How about Stephanie? Where is Stephanie?

His heart starts to slam his chest. He quickly stands up and looks around. He realizes that everything is in such chaos here. Since he is okay, he probably can use his medical training to help these people later on, but right now his priority is to find Stephanie.

While he is looking for her, he notices that the bus that carried them earlier is rolled to the side and only half of the bus remains. The roof and the front part of the bus are missing and he can see some of the seats inside. That doesn't look good. Only a loud explosion can cause the bus to be in that state.

Is this a terrorist attack?

His stomach feels uneasy right away.

He quickly walks around and tries to find Stephanie. The other people he finds on the ground don't look good at all. Some are covered in blood. And some have missing limbs. Damn.

He needs to find Stephanie very quickly. It's hard to find people when everything is very dark and smoky like this. But Stephanie must not be very far from him as they sat together in the bus.

Then finally he sees her.

There she is, lying on the street. Raphael quickly runs towards her.

"Steph!" He kneels down beside her. She is unconscious but is still alive, thank God. He carefully positions her body flat on the ground. Her limbs are also still there. Her face and clothes are full of dust but there is no blood.

He quickly examines her. Her airway is intact, but she is breathing weakly. Her pulse is also weak and she does not respond to him. This is not good. He tries to examine her pupillary response but it is hard in the dark like this.

He looks for the available paramedics. "Help!" he shouts. But all the paramedics look very busy. He knows that they probably will prioritize people with hemorrhage and missing limbs first. As much as he wants to help them, too, he doesn't want to leave Stephanie unattended. Plus, he doesn't know where his backpack is and he doesn't have the kits to tend to their wounds. So, he is just desperately waiting for the paramedics to come to them while keeping his one hand on Stephanie's wrist to ensure that she still has a pulse and his other hand holding her hand.

A few minutes later, two paramedics bring a stretcher. They also secure Stephanie's neck with a neck brace. Finally, he gets into the ambulance with them.

Inside the ambulance, the paramedics start working on Stephanie. It takes him a lot of self-control not to interfere. Plus, they are speaking in Hebrew (or is it in Arabic?) among themselves. So, he doesn't really understand.

The paramedics hook her into a heart monitor and give her oxygen. Other than some minor cuts, Stephanie doesn't seem to sustain any major injuries or bleeding. But her blood pressure is very low. There could be internal bleeding somewhere.

Once they arrive at the hospital, a team of nurses and doctors quickly take over. He stands close by to make sure that Stephanie gets appropriate care before a nurse pulls him aside.

"Sir, are you injured, too?" the young nurse asks.

"No, I don't think so. Could you please make sure this patient is thoroughly examined? She needs a CT and x-ray as soon as possible. She has been unconscious for quite some time. Her pupil response also looks alarming. We need to consult a neurologist or a neurosurgeon, too," Raphael starts to ramble in panic.

"Don't worry about that. She is in good care. But you are bleeding, too, sir."

"What?"

He glances over himself. Now with the sufficient light in the hospital ER, he can see that the right sleeve of his jacket is full of blood. Back in the ambulance, nobody noticed because everybody was busy with Stephanie. Where is the blood coming from? Is this his own blood? He also feels sticky and warm on his shoulder. He inserts his hand beneath his shirt to examine his shoulder. Once he takes out his hand, his palm is full of blood.

"Please lie down here." The nurse points out at the gurney beside them.

Before he can lie down, he passes out again.

@@@

Tel Aviv

Israel Day 7

Raphael opens his eyes. For a moment he feels disoriented.

He is lying down in a bed. The light in the room is bright. Plus, he can see the sunlight coming from the window. He has to squint his eyes as the light is too strong. It makes him a bit dizzy, too.

"Raphael!"

Before he can process his surroundings, he can feel someone is hugging him.

"Gaby?" He tries to speak although his voice sounds muffled. He realizes that he has an oxygen mask over his face.

"Yes. Thank God you are awake," Gaby says.

Now Raphael sees her face clearer. Gaby is not alone in the room. Michelle, André, and Guillaume are also there. Where is he?

He looks at his surroundings. He is in a hospital room and is lying down in a hospital bed. He is wearing a hospital gown and his arm is hooked with an IV. He is also attached to a heart monitor.

Now he starts to remember what happened. He remembered that he and Stephanie were on the bus before he heard an explosion. And suddenly they were on the street. He remembered he was in the ambulance with Stephanie.

Where is Stephanie? Is she alive?

Raphael tries to get up quickly. But André and Guillaume push him back to the bed.

"Hey, relax, Raphael," André says.

Raphael takes off his oxygen mask. "Where is Stephanie? I need to see her." His voice sounds very hoarse. But he doesn't care.

"Raphael, calm down. She is alive, okay? But you need to calm down," Guillaume says while pushing his shoulder to the bed. "Michelle, can you please call the doctor?"

"Sure." Michelle leaves the room.

"What day is it?" Raphael asks them.

"Thursday. You were brought in last night. And you were unconscious the whole night," André says.

"I brought myself in. And Stephanie. See? I am strong enough to wake up. Let me get off and see her."

Guillaume shakes his head. "It's not you who decide, Raphael. The doctor said you were injured pretty badly, too. A shrapnel shard got into your right shoulder and you lost a lot of blood. You also bruised your hip. And you inhaled a lot of smoke."

Raphael slides his hospital gown's right sleeve and sees that his right shoulder is bandaged. He doesn't feel any pain, though, but then he looks at the IV bag and realizes that they must have given him a painkiller.

After that a doctor and a nurse come into the room. The first thing he asks them is, "How's my friend? Is she okay?"

"Relax, young man." The doctor throws him a smile. Raphael reads his ID badge.

"Listen, Dr. Hamad, I am fine now so please discharge me right away," he says without patience.

They ignore him and instead start checking on him. The nurse adjusts his IV. He realizes that she is the same nurse that he saw yesterday.

After they finish checking on him, Dr. Hamad repeats what Guillaume says about the extent of his injuries. And he has to stay for at least a few more days for observation.

"Okay, whatever, Doc. But I really need to see my friend. How is she?"

Dr. Hamad sighs. "She had a brain injury. They operated on her last night. Now, she is still in the ICU."

Raphael feels a hit in his stomach.

No. This cannot be happening. Not to Stephanie.

He quickly pulls out the electrodes that are attached to his chest. He has to see her as soon as possible. He tries to stand but then he feels pain in his hips when putting his weight on his right leg. He almost loses balance before Guillaume catches him.

"We'll bring you to Stephanie, okay? But you need to calm down, Raphael," Guillaume says.

"Let's get him a wheelchair," Dr. Hamad tells the nurse.

A few minutes later, Guillaume pushes his wheelchair while André is pushing the IV. Raphael realizes that he is still wearing the hospital gown with nothing underneath it. But he doesn't care. His mind is occupied with Stephanie.

As only three people are allowed in the ICU at a time, Gaby and Michelle decide to wait outside and let Raphael, André, and Guillaume enter first.

Finally, they enter the ICU, where Stephanie is lying in one of the beds, unconscious. Her body is also hooked with a lot of equipment. What makes Raphael even more hopeless is when he sees that she is intubated. That could mean that the damage to her brain is pretty severe to the point that she cannot breathe on her own.

Two other doctors are standing beside Stephanie's bed. The older one must be an attending, while the younger one must be a resident.

Raphael tries to stand up but almost falls again. André and Guillaume help him stand up and support both his arms.

"Doc, how's my friend?" Raphael asks both doctors.

The younger resident steps in, "She sustained a traumatic brain injury. We operated on her last night. Now she is in a coma. I am sorry."

Raphael tries to remain calm. He takes several deep breaths. He is trying to digest what they say.

"How long was it since the operation?" he asks.

"More than seven hours ago," the resident replies.

"Which part of the brain is injured? And what was the surgery for?"

"There was a hematoma in the temporal lobe. We removed the blood clots."

"And the GCS score?" GCS stands for Glasgow Coma Scale, which is a common tool to assess the level of consciousness of a patient.

Both of the doctors are looking at each other.

"Are you a doctor?" The attending asks him.

"Yes."

"Her score is five," the resident replies.

Raphael almost falls again if André and Guillaume are not supporting him.

Five? With the highest score of fifteen and the lowest score of three, a five doesn't look very good at all. She has a severe traumatic brain injury with poor prognosis. Raphael cannot accept this.

Ignoring the pain in his hips, he moves closer to Stephanie and assesses her himself. He calls her names multiple times and pinches her with his fingernails to get a response. There is no eye response. He doesn't expect any verbal response as she is intubated.

Raphael almost gives up before something promising happens.

He pinches her shoulder and her elbow bends slowly and the arm comes across the body.

She displays abnormal flexion to pain! This is better than no response at all.

"Also, at least her PRS is zero," the resident continues. PRS stands of Pupil Reactivity Score. A score of zero means both pupils are reactive to lights.

Although Raphael trusts him, he wants to check this good news himself. He takes the resident's penlight and examines Stephanie's pupil reaction himself. He sighs with relief when both pupils constrict. If one or both pupils are not reactive, it will further decrease the GCS score. This gives him a slight hope that she may still survive, although they don't know if her life is still going to be the same or not after this.

However, at the end, he has to agree with the neurosurgery resident's GCS-P (GCS Pupil Score) assessment of five. He suddenly feels very powerless. He looks at Stephanie again. She looks like she is just sleeping peacefully. But he knows that she is in a much worse condition than just sleeping. There is no certainty that she will wake up at all.

Why did this happen to her? What did she do to deserve this?

Raphael would give everything up just to see Stephanie wake up again. He wants to see her smile again, he wants her to hug him, he wants to see her full energy during workout, and he wants to see her playing the violin again. But will that happen? He doesn't know.

These extreme sadness and powerlessness start to affect his body again. He feels pain in his stomach and he feels nauseous. He starts to lose his balance again.

"Raphael!" André and Guillaume quickly catch him and put him back on the wheelchair. After that, the three of them are just watching Stephanie without words.

Once outside the ICU, Gaby and Michelle grab his hands to give him moral support. But nothing that his sisters and his friends do can make him feel better.

He buries his face in his arms and sobs quietly.

Chapter 24

Tel Aviv

For the next few hours, Raphael feels numb. He doesn't feel his own physical pain. He tries not to focus on his emotional pain. But he feels the emptiness.

He knows that he should be grateful that his sisters and his best friends are here with him. He is impressed that they found him in the hospital very quickly. Guillaume told him that André and Gaby could sense when he was in danger during the explosion. Once he and Stephanie didn't show up at their hotel and were unreachable, they followed the news and discovered that there was an explosion near Tel Aviv. They assumed that Raphael and Stephanie were one of the victims and started making calls to the hospitals near the explosion site.

Luckily, Raphael still has his identification with him. His wallet is saved in the back pocket of his jeans. When he passed out yesterday, the hospital could identify him. However, the rest of his belongings were blown up during the explosion, including his passport. Luckily, Guillaume has already made contact with the Canadian embassy in Tel Aviv to request a new passport for him. Guillaume also gave him a new phone, as his phone was severely damaged during the explosion.

He can also enjoy this VIP room in the hospital, thanks to André and Guillaume who upgraded his room. Without them, he has to handle all these tedious administrative things himself, which he doesn't think that he has the capacity at this point.

Gaby and Michelle have also informed their parents. His mom and dad were panicking when they heard the news. They booked tickets to Tel Aviv right away. They will arrive in the next two days.

Guillaume has also contacted Stephanie's parents. Raphael doesn't know how he got their contact information, but as an artist manager, Guillaume is very resourceful. Raphael has no idea when Stephanie's parents are going to arrive. He doesn't know what he will tell them. He feels ashamed that he failed to protect Stephanie.

"Do we know who the perpetrator is?" Michelle asks. Raphael is too sad about Stephanie to the point that he doesn't even care who caused this attack.

Guillaume sighs, "We cannot know for sure. The first guess will be the Palestinians, as the explosion is on the Israel side. But it could also be Israelis who tried to blame the Palestinians. Or it could be the civil war between Israel themselves. You know, Orthodox versus Reformed Jewish."

"I am sick of all of this. Why can't people live together in peace?" Gaby says.

"We cannot judge really, because we don't live here. We don't know what they have been through," André says wisely.

They chat a bit more but then André seems to notice that Raphael is not in the mood to talk, and he suggests that they go back to the hotel and leave Raphael alone to rest. But Gaby has a different plan.

"Raphael, can I stay with you here tonight? I will sleep on the couch," Gaby says.

"Yes, of course. It will be uncomfortable, though." Raphael actually really appreciates that Gaby is willing to stay. If the four of them stay over, it will be too much. But if it is just Gaby, he actually likes that idea. Raphael feels like he can just be himself in front of Gaby.

After André, Guillaume, and Michelle leave, now it's time to really talk heart-to-heart with Gaby.

"Raphael, I went through the same thing as you last year, remember? After André got a heart surgery. I may not know exactly how you feel, but I can relate. You don't have to go through this alone, Raphael."

"Thanks, Gabs."

After that he starts telling Gaby the story between him and Stephanie from the first time they met until now. From the moment she showed up in the ER in his hospital, their time together in North Korea, and then Dubai, and then their challenging hike in Israel.

"I ask myself, why did this happen to us? Right when it's going very well between us. Right when we start to see our future together. It's so unfair. I remember you experienced the same thing with André. How did you deal with this?" Raphael asks. He wipes tears in his eyes. He doesn't care how he must look weak in front of his sister.

"Yes, I also felt it was unfair in the beginning. We were just falling in love, but suddenly there was a high possibility that he may not have survived and I wouldn't be able to see him or talk to him again. It was heartbreaking. But then, when I thought about it, even if André didn't survive, wasn't I already lucky enough to meet him in the first place? Out of many women that he could meet, or many men I could meet, fate brought us together. I told myself I shouldn't be too greedy. Nothing in this world could last forever. We just have to appreciate when it happens, but be ready when it has to end.

"Out of thousands of patients that you could possibly encounter, it was Stephanie who showed up in the ER that day. Out of hundreds of doctors that she could meet, it was you who were assigned to treat her. Wasn't it fate? But at that time, did you ask, why is it me who got lucky to meet Stephanie? Now, are you entitled to complain why the explosion happened to you and Stephanie instead of to other couples?"

Raphael digests Gaby's words. She is right. But it is so much easier said than done. It makes sense logically. But he has emotion too, although he relies more on logic.

"It's hard, Gabs."

"I know, Raphael. I know."

@@@

Tel Aviv
Israel, Day 8

The next day looks better. The doctor informs them that Stephanie has made progress. Her motoric response shows withdrawal from pain stimuli and she opens her eyes in response to pain. That brings the Glasgow Coma Scale score to seven. She still needs to be intubated but at least she is showing progress.

Raphael is very eager to visit her again. But this time he wants to look more presentable. As much as he wants to wear his street clothes, the nurse who checked him up this morning recommended that he keep wearing hospital gown instead of street clothes to make it easy for them. They still have to change the wound dressing on his shoulder as well as hook his arm to the IV. He hates being a patient. But maybe after this he will be more sympathetic towards his patients.

However, to protect his dignity, he sees no reason why he cannot put on his underwear. While Gaby, Michelle, André, and Guillaume are getting breakfast somewhere downstairs, he slowly walks towards his luggage to find his underwear. Again, he is grateful that Guillaume dropped his luggage this morning, so now he has clothes.

With his shoulder and hips still sore, it is hard to bend around. And when he tries to kneel beside the luggage, a sudden sharp pain on his hip gives him a shock until he falls on his butt.

"Damn." He winces in pain.

André, Guillaume, Gaby, and Michelle come at the right time.

"Raphael! What's going on?" Gaby walks towards him panicky.

"I am trying to dress myself up," he says with embarrassment.

"Gabs, Michelle, how about you wait outside while we are helping Raphael?" André says. Raphael is glad that André is very thoughtful.

"Seriously? Do you know that the three of us showered together until he was thirteen?" Michelle says before she and Gaby leave the room.

Guillaume helps him stand up while André helps him dress up.

"Don't feel bad, Raphael. I was on the same boat as you last year, I couldn't put on my own clothes," André says after he finishes helping him.

"Thanks, man." Raphael feels so much better after wearing underwear underneath his hospital gown.

After that, he walks towards the ICU to visit Stephanie. This time, his friends and his sisters give him privacy and leave him alone with Stephanie. Raphael takes a seat beside her bed and examines her carefully.

Stephanie is still looking asleep. He restrains himself not to pinch her to make her open her eyes. If there are no breathing tubes, she could be mistaken as asleep. Although she has made progress this morning, she is still in a coma, which is even worse than vegetative state. But it has only been two days, right? How long is she going to be like this? Another day? A week? A month?

He grabs her hand and starts talking even though she may or may not hear him.

"Steph, I hope you will wake up soon. I miss you so much. I am worried about you. I regret that I didn't show more love or care towards you when you were conscious. Had I known that you would be unconscious like this, I wouldn't have held myself back, you know? I know I may lack confidence in approaching you or expressing my love to you. But please never doubt my feelings towards you. I want to have a future with you, Stephanie. There will be more adventure waiting for us once you regain consciousness..."

Raphael also misses listening to her live violin performance. As such, he takes out his new phone that Guillaume provided and starts playing Dvorak's four romantic pieces, which are Stephanie's favorite pieces—as well as his.

@@@

Tel Aviv
Israel, Day 9

A miracle happens the next morning.

Stephanie has woken up.

When the nurse tells him that morning, he almost cries because he is too happy.

"Fully conscious?" Raphael asks impatiently. He cannot wait to meet her.

"Yes. She is still a bit confused, but yes, she can understand and obey commands. Last night she finally opened her eyes and displayed full motor response. We removed the breathing tube and she can breathe on her own. But again, she looks scared and confused. But it's common for TBI (Traumatic Brain Injury) patients."

"Can I meet her now? Please take this out." Raphael points out his IV. "And help me get dressed please."

Finally, Raphael can wear his regular checkered shirt and jeans. He feels much stronger, healthier, and ready to meet Stephanie. He is also excited that they have moved Stephanie from the ICU to a regular room. Her sudden fast recovery surprises everyone.

They enter a semi-private room which has three beds in it.

Stephanie is sitting on the furthest bed in the corner, looking outside the window. She looks a bit pale but she is awake!

"Steph!" Raphael quickly walks towards her to hug her. He misses her so much. From now on, he will not waste a single second not by her side.

But once he stands by her bed, her reaction is not what he is expecting.

She doesn't seem to be happy or relieved to see him.

She looks surprised and...confused.

He stops approaching her when she backs off a bit.

"Steph? Are you okay?" Raphael asks carefully. He really wants to touch her hands and her face. But he restrains himself.

She looks at him quizzically.

"I am sorry, who are you?"

Chapter 25

Tel Aviv

Raphael is stunned for a second.

How can this be?

"Steph, you don't recognize me?" he asks slowly. He looks at her full of joy and hope. But she looks at him like he is a stranger.

"I... don't, I'm sorry. Everything is so confusing. I am in Israel, right? Why am I here? Did we travel together?" she asks him, trying to find answers.

Raphael is still shocked. Where is the Stephanie that he knows? How come she doesn't remember anything for the past few weeks? Is this woman really Stephanie? She has the exact appearance as Stephanie. But why doesn't she recognize him? Why does she treat him like a stranger?

Yes. She is the same Stephanie who has spent the past three weeks together with him. The fact that she doesn't recognize him hurts him so much.

Could it be amnesia?

Raphael tries to separate his feelings from her condition. It's hard. He feels alone right now.

He takes a deep breath and takes a seat beside her bed.

"Hi Stephanie. My name is Raphael Zhang. Yes, we traveled together for the past three weeks. I am sure the doctors have told you that you have had an accident and you have a head injury. That's why you are confused now." He tries to put aside his feelings and treats her as a professional instead of a lover. It hurts him a lot to do this.

Stephanie doesn't say anything. Raphael can understand that she must feel overwhelmed right now. He knows that he should call a doctor, but he is curious about the extent of her memory loss.

Before he begins, he glances at her monitor that displays her vital signs. Everything looks okay. Her eyes are also focused. "Stephanie, I have medical training, too, in Canada. Do you mind if I ask you several questions before I call the doctors who are in charge of you?"

Stephanie is trying to assess his sincerity before finally nodding. He will not do a cognitive test or neurology exam on her, as she is not his patient. He will just ask questions that are personally relevant for him.

"First of all, is your head okay? Do you have a headache?" Raphael asks.

"Yes, but it's still bearable." She touches her head automatically.

"Can you tell me your full name please?"

"Stephanie Adams."

"Where and when were you born?"

"Toronto, August eighth." She also mentions the year.

"Where do you live?"

"Toronto."

"Where are you now?"

"Umm... I know we are in the hospital. I initially thought I was in a hospital in Toronto. But everything here is written in Hebrew. So, am I in Israel?"

"Yes. We are in Tel Aviv. Do you remember when you were admitted to the hospital?"

She shakes her head.

"What was the last event you can recall before the incident?"

It takes her sometimes to think.

"It's all blurred in my head. I remember working out in the gym in my condo in Toronto. I visited my clients—I am a music therapist, by the way," she finally says. Raphael is surprised by her answer. Her memory loss seems to be quite serious.

"Did you recall you got your arm injured with broken glass while visiting a client and you brought yourself to the ER in

Toronto?" He starts to go off-script and asks more personal questions.

She thinks for a few seconds and then shakes her head. Raphael feels extreme sadness and emptiness again. She doesn't recall the moment they met the first time. He feels uneasiness in his stomach again.

"What month and year is it now?" he continues with the standard questions.

"Umm..." She thinks hard again. "September?" Stephanie guesses the month wrong but at least she guesses the year correctly.

Raphael has expected this. She seems not to remember anything for the past few months.

"December," Raphael clarifies.

Stephanie looks scared, "It's December already? How come...?" She seems very discouraged, so he decides to throw something familiar for her.

"Who is the current prime minister of Canada?"

"Justin Trudeau."

"Who is your favorite composer?"

Stephanie looks at him as she doesn't expect this question. "Dvorak."

"What is the national anthem of North Korea?" Raphael is not sure himself why he asks these questions. To trigger her recent memories?

"Aegukka."

"Have you ever done skydiving before?"

"Skydiving? No. Is this a common question?"

He shouldn't have asked these questions. It's just going to hurt him more. But he keeps going.

"Is this your first time in Israel?"

"No."

"When was the last time you visited Israel, and what did you do?"

"Two years ago. I hiked from Nazareth to Capernaum."

"By yourself?'

"Yes."

Raphael is not going to ask the next question, 'How many times have you done this hike?'. She will say, 'once', and he doesn't want to accept the reality that she remembers nothing about the hike that they did together. He decides to close the interview with the last question.

"What is my name?"

"Raphael Zhang," she says without hesitation. It makes him sad how he longed to hear her saying his name in a more intimate way instead of like a stranger like just now.

He decides that he has gathered enough information to conclude that Stephanie has a post-traumatic retrograde amnesia. She lost her recent memories but at least she retains long-term memory, as well as the ability to form new memories. It hurts that she doesn't remember anything about him, although he knows that it is not her fault.

He cannot continue anymore.

"Okay. I will call a doctor now and let you rest. Get well soon, Stephanie." He stands up.

"Wait."

He turns towards her.

"I... I'm sorry, I feel so foreign now. Can you please tell me what's going on? Who are you, Raphael Zhang? How do we know each other? Are we friends?"

Raphael puts his hand on her shoulder, a gesture that he thinks is still considered professional.

"Stephanie, I don't want to overwhelm you with details that you don't remember. You need to take it easy. Get some rest. You have just had a big accident. Take one step at a time."

Then, he leaves.

Raphael is finally back to his room. He has notified the doctors in charge of Stephanie that she seems to have retrograde amnesia. They are doing a full examination on her right now. He really hopes that the brain injury is not too severe. Other than her memory loss, she appears to be recovering very well.

What about him? He feels numb.

It will take some time for him to process what happened to Stephanie. He should be grateful that Stephanie is still alive and is able to talk. But without her memory, what does it mean for their relationship now? He still loves her very much, even when she doesn't remember who he is and what happened to them. But what about her?

There is a possibility that her memory may gradually come back. But there is also a possibility that it will be lost forever.

Imagining this makes him feel sick in the stomach again. He has never felt this empty in his life. He has had too much expectation in their relationship. Now he feels like he is starting from scratch again.

He looks outside the window. Stephanie is right. Everything seems very foreign. There are olive trees everywhere. Everything is written in Hebrew. The buildings are older than in Toronto. He can imagine how scary it must be for Stephanie when she finds herself in a foreign country without remembering how she got here.

He has to be selfless. He has to think of the best course of action for her, and not for himself. Right now, what he wants to do is just to look her in the eyes and tell her what happened between them in the past three weeks. He wouldn't spare any details. He would tell her that he loves her and she loves him, too. But how would she take it? She cannot just love him out of the blue without any memory of falling in love with him. He doesn't want her to be overwhelmed, or worse, to feel obligated to love him. Therefore, he decides that the best course of action will be to let her recover her memory naturally, which may or may not happen.

A few minutes later, André, Guillaume, Gaby, and Michelle arrive.

They look very happy and they bring Stephanie's luggage and violin as well. He texted them this morning that Stephanie has woken up but he hasn't told them about her memory loss.

"Raphael? Why are you here? Aren't you supposed to be with Stephanie?" Guillaume says while handing him his new passport.

Raphael doesn't answer at first. He retrieves his new passport from Guillaume unenthusiastically.

"Is there something wrong?" André asks.

Raphael tells them what he found this morning about Stephanie's condition. After he finishes, they look at him in shock and disbelief.

"I am so sorry, Raphael," Gaby says sympathetically.

Michelle puts her hand on his shoulder. "Wait a second. Look at the bright side. She is awake, no other health problems other than her amnesia. And this amnesia, isn't it only temporary?"

"I don't know. She was in a coma for three days, the injury to the brain was pretty severe. She may or may not recover her memory."

"But she is functioning well, right? Like she remembers all other details except for the past few months. Her intelligence and decision-making skills are not impaired, right?" Michelle continues.

"I don't think so, but I didn't perform a full examination on her. Her doctors are doing it right now," Raphael says flatly.

Nobody says anything for a while. They probably realize how devastated Raphael is.

"So, what are you going to do now? Are you going to tell her what happened for the past three weeks?" Guillaume asks. Raphael shakes his head.

"Can we see her, too? Maybe seeing our faces could trigger some memories?" André asks.

"You can. But let's not overwhelm her. She has suffered enough."

"And I will bring her violin. I hope it will help her feel better," Gaby says while picking up Stephanie's violin.

As expected, Stephanie is looking at André, Guillaume, Gaby, and Michelle with confusion. Raphael feels hopeless again. But when André starts speaking Korean with her, she can reply fluently.

"How do you know I speak Korean?" Stephanie asks André in Korean. She seems surprised.

"A lot of things have happened to you in the past few weeks or months. And all of us are your new friends. It's understandable if you don't remember us. But don't stress out about it," André says kindly in Korean.

"I am sorry."

"Don't be. It's not your fault." André switches back to English. "We can start all over again. My name is André. This is my fiancé Gaby. These are Raphael, Guillaume, and Michelle, my best friends. Raphael, Gaby, and Michelle are siblings too."

Stephanie nods. "And how did we know each other?"

André looks at Raphael for a second.

"Raphael was the one who introduced you to us. You knew Raphael first."

Stephanie now looks at Raphael. A sad expression is written on her face. So is his face. But Raphael doesn't say anything.

"Also, don't be surprised if we know a few things, or maybe a lot of things about you. We know that you are very adventurous and very sporty," Guillaume adds.

"And you like watching Korean dramas and listening to K-pop. Just like me," Michelle says.

"And you are an awesome musician," Gaby says. "Also, here, I bring something for you to cheer you up." Gaby hands the violin to Stephanie.

Stephanie looks at the violin with joy and gratitude. She accepts the violin carefully and opens the box. It's the first time she looks happy since she woke up. Raphael starts to feel tears in his eyes. But he tries to keep his composure.

"Do you want to play it?" André asks.

"Yes."

"Come with me, I found a perfect place. Are you okay to walk?"

Before Stephanie can reply, Raphael jumps in. "I will get a wheelchair. Her muscles must still be very weak."

After that, André takes them to a hallway where there is an upright piano. Raphael pushes Stephanie's wheelchair carefully from her room to the hallway. Michelle also wraps a coat around Stephanie to cover her back, as she is only wearing a hospital gown. Looking at his best friends and his sisters taking care of Stephanie makes him feel less alone.

"Okay. Anytime you are ready, Steph." André sits behind the piano.

Stephanie is looking at her violin. The violin that was gifted to her by the North Koreans. It's sad that she doesn't remember that moment.

She tries out her violin by moving the bow against the strings. André helps her tune the violin.

"I am not sure what to play," she says.

This may be a good opportunity to trigger some of her memories back. Also to confirm that she still retains her violin skills, which means that the brain injury is not that severe at this point.

"Would you mind playing the third movement of Dvorak's four romantic pieces?" Raphael says suddenly. Last time in Dubai,

Stephanie and André played the second movement of the pieces. He is very eager to hear her play the third movement.

"Okay." Stephanie nods and starts to play.

Romance.

The tempo is Allegro appassionato.

The melody starts fresh. It sounds sweet, hopeful, and passionate. Stephanie plays it full of passion, too. She finally looks like herself again. She appears very comfortable with her violin. Raphael wishes that he was the violin that she is holding right now.

When she is playing the piece, he remembers their hike from Nazareth to Capernaum. The villages, the green fields that they passed, olive trees, valleys, mountains, as well as the Sea of Galilee. In the middle of the piece, the melody turns sad and thrilling. It sounds like they are facing a difficult challenge. It makes him remember the challenging part of their hike during the thunderstorm from Kibbutz Lavi to Moshav Arbel. And also like right now. Especially with Stephanie's condition.

But the closing of the piece is back to the sweet and hopeful melody. Raphael wants to believe that there is still hope between him and Stephanie.

"Do you want me to continue to the fourth movement?" Stephanie asks Raphael after she finishes the third movement.

He doesn't reply at first. The answer would be no. He knows how sad the fourth movement is. But he wants to keep listening to Stephanie. And the fourth movement really represents how he feels right now.

"Yes, please," he finally replies.

Stephanie and André start the fourth movement.

Elegy.

The tempo is Larghetto instead of Allegro. This is the longest and the saddest out of the other three movements. This music makes him sad instantaneously. It's like saying goodbye to the memory that Stephanie has lost. The beautiful memory that they have created for the past three weeks.

Raphael doesn't know how to process this sadness. He holds his tears until the music ends.

"How are you feeling now?" André asks after they are back into his room. Gaby and Michelle escorted Stephanie back into her room and haven't come back until now. They must be chatting with her now. Raphael has warned his sisters not to overwhelm Stephanie as she is still recovering. He also told Gaby and Michelle not to mention anything about his relationship with Stephanie. He wants her to remember it on her own, not because someone told her.

While Guillaume is taking care of his hospital paperwork downstairs, it is only he and André in the room.

"I am not sure. I know I should be grateful that Stephanie's recovery is pretty quick. She retains her language skills and her ability to play the violin. But her memory loss... Maybe I am also selfish." He looks at the ground.

"Gaby told me about your relationship with her for the past three weeks. It's not easy to just forget it all. Don't feel bad about being selfish. If I were you, I would be extremely sad, too."

"At one point, I told Stephanie that I may have been mixing love and pleasure when I was with her. And one way to tell whether it's love or pleasure is when I have seen the worst of her and I still love her."

"Do you still love her?"

"Yes, very much. But that's the problem. I realize I love her regardless of what happened. What if she won't feel the same anymore?"

"I can see that she is still the same person. She may not remember us, but the way she behaves is the same as before. You guys may fall in love quickly because of this trip. But regardless of the settings, I am sure that she will fall in love with you again, sooner or later, because you are also still who you are."

"I hope you are right, André. But how long should I wait? And what if she falls in love with someone else?"

"Wait for her as long as you are willing to. Even if she doesn't end up with you, isn't it what love is? Letting the person go if that's what they want?"

Chapter 26

Tel Aviv
Israel, Day 9

The past few hours have been very chaotic for Stephanie. She woke up last night finding herself in the hospital in Israel! The doctors and nurses speak in Hebrew, the language that she recognizes right away due to her Jewish mom, although she cannot speak it herself.

They told her that she had been in a bombing accident near Tel Aviv. In the beginning she thought she went crazy. Why was she even in Tel Aviv? But after that the doctor said that she injured her head and it's common to be confused and have some memory loss. They said they would perform a full checkup on her in the morning.

But this morning, things got more bizarre. A very handsome Asian man, probably in his late twenties or early thirties, visited her. His face was full of worries but full of joy when seeing and approaching her. He behaved like they knew each other very well. But the problem is, she doesn't know him. That was the first time she met him.

After that his demeanor changed one hundred and eighty degrees. He looked extremely sad and more withdrawn, although he was still very caring. He introduced himself as Raphael Zhang. He told her that they have traveled together for the past three weeks. He asked her a series of questions. Some of the questions seemed to be common medical assessment questions, but some of the questions seemed to be tailored specifically for her. And he seemed to know the answer already.

Who is Raphael Zhang?

After that a team of doctors performed a full physical and mental examination on her. They asked similar questions to

Raphael's. However, she felt much more comfortable with Raphael. Although she doesn't know him, he gave off a warm and familiar vibe that she didn't get from other doctors. Maybe because Raphael is also from Canada.

After she did a CT scan, blood work, and other uncomfortable medical test, she returned to her room and was visited by a bunch of people she didn't recognize either. She was relieved that Raphael was there, too, although he didn't talk much.

These people seemed to be very nice. She was instantly at ease and put her guard down. Also, she noticed that they were all very sophisticated-looking. André, the one who led the conversation, seemed very polite. He is kind of a mix between Caucasian and Asian. He speaks English with a slight French accent, and he speaks Korean, too. They must have conversed in Korean in the past, although she didn't remember. Guillaume must also be a French-Canadian based on his accent. He is a typical Caucasian with blonde hair and blue eyes. There was also Michelle, a stunningly beautiful Asian lady who bears resemblance to Raphael, and Gaby, another Asian lady who is also very pretty, sweet, and cute.

Who are these people?

While they were talking to her, she kept glancing at Raphael, who seemed so depressed. Was it because of her condition?

Stephanie was so relieved when Gaby handed her a violin. She finally found something familiar. After that André brought them to the hallway where there was a piano and he accompanied her. She played Dvorak's third and four movements of the four romantic pieces, as requested by Raphael. By now she realizes that she must have shared with him details about her, including her favorite composers and favorite pieces. He seems to know her in and out. Now she is wondering, are she and Raphael perhaps more than friends?

Were they lovers?

Raphael's sisters, Michelle and Gaby, are also very caring towards her. After her performance, they stayed a bit with her. Michelle helped Stephanie brush her hair and Gaby kept praising her violin performance genuinely. Talking to these kind strangers gave her a huge comfort, despite her headache and head wound.

Suddenly, she finds Guillaume standing by the curtain that separates her bed and other patients' beds. "Steph, can I come in?"

"Hi, Guillaume, yes please come in. What's up?" Stephanie is a bit disappointed when she finds out that Guillaume is alone and Raphael is not there.

"Here is your new passport and new phone. Don't ask me how I got this. But long story short, you traveled with Raphael first in the beginning, and he kept a photocopy of your passport." Guillaume hands her the new passport and phone carefully. Stephanie doesn't even think about her passport yet at this point, but she is very grateful that someone did this for her.

"Wow, thanks so much, Guillaume. I really appreciate it."

"By the way, the five of us including Raphael will fly back to Canada tomorrow."

Stephanie feels like her heart skips a beat. Although they are still strangers to her at this point, she doesn't understand why she feels like she really needs their presence. Especially Raphael.

"Oh, okay." She tries to hide her disappointment.

"I talked to the doctors and they said that they wanted to keep you here for the next few days for further observation," Guillaume continues. Imagining that she still has to spend some time in this hospital alone scares her out. She hopes that her parents are here. But they are far away in Toronto. She looks at her new phone and makes a note to call them after this.

"But we are not mean. Instead of leaving you here alone by yourself, look who I brought."

Guillaume draws the curtain behind him, and two people that she loves the most appear in front of her.

Her mom and dad.

Before she can react, they hug her tightly.

Finally, although she hasn't returned home, she feels at home immediately in the presence of her parents. She feels safe.

"Stephanie, you cannot imagine how scared I was when I heard the news," Her mom says.

"Yeah, me too. I am glad that you are safe," Her dad says.

She starts crying. These past couple days have been very hard. She is longing for familiarity.

Guillaume gives her a sympathetic look before he leaves to give them some private family time.

And Stephanie realizes that today is Christmas day.

@@@

Raphael is finally discharged from the hospital that evening. He counts this as a Christmas gift. As much as he wishes that he could be by Stephanie's side, he knows that right now she is busy with her parents and he is aware that he is probably still a 'stranger' to her. As such, he doesn't want to creep her out by following her all the time. So, he returns to his hotel with his sisters and friends.

When he returns to the hotel, there is a surprise that has been waiting for him.

His parents are already inside the suite welcoming him.

He doesn't waste a single second. He walks towards them and hugs them both.

He feels very relieved. Since he was in North Korea, there were times when he was not sure if he would see them again. But now they are there in front of him. They reunite on Christmas Day.

His mom starts to cry.

"Raphael, can you please stop making me worried?" she says while hugging him tight.

"Yes, Mom. I think the adventure was a bit too much this time," he acknowledges.

"Raphael, don't make my blood pressure go up again, please," his dad says.

He knows that his dad has a high blood pressure due to the stress from managing his own law firm. He feels guilty for making him worried.

"Yes, Dad."

After that, they all go to the Old Jaffa area to have dinner. This is his parents' first time in Israel. He wishes that they can enjoy this country in a better situation, but their goal is just to spend time with him and make sure that he is okay. Tomorrow, all of them will return to Canada.

Raphael tells his parents everything about his trip starting from North Korea, Dubai, and finally to Israel. He also mentions Stephanie and gets carried away with his emotion a little bit. His parents look at him sympathetically.

That night, they enjoy a beautiful night walk around Old Jaffa. Although he is still thinking about Stephanie all the time, with the support from his friends and family, he is hopeful that he can go through this all.

@@@

Tel Aviv,
Israel, Day 10

Stephanie feels her heart beat faster when Raphael visits her to say goodbye the next day.

Although she feels better with her parents beside her, she cannot deny that she has been waiting for him, too. She has so many questions to ask him, but she is not sure where and how to start. The way that he behaves and cares about her makes her very curious about what kind of life they have had together before she lost her memory.

She has also met his parents and they both are very kind, just like Raphael's friends and sisters. Now her parents are talking with his parents outside of the room.

"So, how do you feel today?" Raphael asks while it's just the two of them.

"I feel better."

"No headache or nausea?"

"Sometimes, but it's not that bad."

After that he asks her if he can take a look at the surgical wound in her head and the wounds on her knees, which she lets him. She doesn't remember how she got the wounds on her knees.

"Did I fall?" she asks him while pointing at her knees. The wounds have healed well. Now it looks like scrapes.

"Yes."

"Will you eventually tell me what happened for the past three weeks? Or what happened between us?"

Raphael looks at her deeply in the eyes.

"Steph, what happened for the past three weeks is something I am going to cherish forever. I have never been that happy and alive before. However, if I tell you what happened while you have no memory about it, it would be like listening to someone else's story instead of your own story. I am afraid it will overwhelm you. Therefore, it is better to wait until your memory returns on its own, so that you won't feel 'forced' to feel certain things towards me or towards our memory."

She doesn't answer him at first. She is digesting his words.

"So that's it then? I would never see you again, after all the things you and your friends have done towards me?"

"I will let you resume your normal life after you return to Canada. I will need some time to process everything that happened. It was very hard for me when I saw you get injured and lose your memory. But I will certainly hope that we will see each other again."

"Okay, then."

"Although I didn't tell you what happened, I think there is nothing wrong with telling you how I feel about you..."

"You... feel something about me?"

"Yes." Then, Raphael hands her a letter in an envelope. "Last night, I wrote this down. Please read it after I leave. And you will know what to do. I decided to write this instead of telling you in person so that you can re-read it and remember it longer. Also, I don't want to scare you out with my confession while you have no memory of me." He looks sad when saying it.

Stephanie is looking at the letter that he handed her. She feels genuinely touched already, even though she hasn't read the letter.

"Thank you very much, Raphael. I am sorry if my memory loss is giving you a hard time. You seem like a really good person. So do your sisters and friends. Thank you for your support. It would be scarier for me if you guys weren't there," Stephanie says.

"You are welcome. You deserve it, Steph. You are a very good person, too. And don't feel bad about losing your memory. It's not your fault at all."

Although he is technically still a stranger, she feels very comfortable with him already. She finds him very understanding. Even though she doesn't know how close they were before this incident happened, it must have been very sad to see someone close to you didn't recognize and remember you because she lost her memory. She resists the urge to hug him before he leaves.

He seems to read her mind. He rises from his seat and wraps his arms around her.

"Goodbye, Steph. We will see each other again in Canada. In the meantime, please get plenty of rest and get well soon."

Then, he kisses her forehead.

Once Raphael leaves, Stephanie feels hollow in her chest. She doesn't know why. She has only known Raphael for two days. But he has given her a huge comfort.

She quickly opens and reads his letter.

Hi Steph,

I write this letter to tell you how I felt for the past few weeks. I am usually a very confident person. I have no trouble confessing my feelings in person. However, when it comes to you, I am not sure why I am no longer the confident person I used to be. Also, I think finding out what happened between us through a letter is less overwhelming than hearing it from me in person.

I wouldn't get into too much detail, but long story short, we traveled together to North Korea, Dubai, and then Israel for the past few weeks. Our trip together is really one of the best moments in my life.

In North Korea, I started to notice you. I realized that you were very different from other girls that I know. You were not obsessed with your appearance or pictures. You dressed up like a tom-boy but I found it very unique. You were friends with other guys and I can see that you are such a fun person to be with, either as a friend or more than that. At that time, I didn't know yet. But since then, I started talking to you more. At some point, I heard you play the violin for the first time. It really melted my heart.

Then, my friends invited both of us to Dubai. I was glad that you were willing to join us. I saw that you also got along really well with my sisters and my friends. You helped André fight his depression and anxiety. Thanks to you, he started doing things that he liked again. Guillaume also really treasured you as his gym buddy. I noticed that he was even more motivated working out with you than with me. Gaby and Michelle also really like you because they can see that you make me happy. At some point, you also helped me overcome my trauma and you were always there for me. I think it was in Dubai where I started to fall for you.

After that we continued our trip to Israel. It was in Jerusalem when I finally had the courage to confess how I feel about you. I felt very relieved. I am very hopeful about our relationship and future together. We made such a great team. We were each other's biggest physical and emotional support especially during our hike. I can see that this will translate into real life as well.

Steph, don't feel bad about losing your memory. It doesn't change the fact that you have brought so much meaning and happiness into my life as well as my friends and family. Just because you don't have any memories of it doesn't mean that it didn't happen. Even after you woke up, you are still the Stephanie that I knew.

Aside from your memory loss, I am relieved that you don't sustain any other serious injuries. We should be grateful. Now what you need to do is focus on getting better and resume your normal life in Canada. As much as I want to come and meet you as soon as you return, I will resist this temptation. I want to give you some space and time to think about what you want to do about us. Whatever your decision is, I will respect that. I enclose my contact information if you need to reach me.

Also, at some point, we made a promise that we will go hiking to Devil's Thumb Mountain in Lake Louise, Alberta, next summer. If you decide that there is a hope between us, please meet me at the summit at around noon on June seventh, which will be my thirty-first birthday. Please don't text me in advance if you decide not to come, because I still want to be hopeful until then. Also, please don't text me if you plan to show up, because I want the thrill and adrenaline of waiting for you.

I really treasure our moments together, Steph.

I love you.

Raphael

Six months later...

Chapter 27

Early June
Lake Louise, Alberta

Raphael enjoys breathing the mountain fresh air. He almost reaches the summit of Devil's Thumb. It takes him less than three hours from the Fairmont Chateau Lake Louise, which is the starting point of the hike, up to this point. Right now, he is scrambling up the final steep section of this hike.

There are several other hiking trails in this area which serve all hikers from beginner to advanced. For beginners, they can hike up to Lake Agnes and little Beehives. For intermediate hikers, they can hike up to Big Beehives. For advanced hikers, they can hike up to Devil's Thumb or Plain of Six Glaciers. Along the way, they can see the Lake Louise mountain range on the opposite side. And at certain points, they can see Lake Louise and Fairmont Chateau down below. The view is extremely gorgeous and feels unreal.

Guillaume and Michelle decide to skip the hike and canoe at the Lake Louise instead. André and Gaby also hike until Big Beehives but they don't hike with him because he is way faster than them.

And he needs to reach Devil's Thumb summit at noon.

The past six months have not been easy for Raphael. Once he returned to Canada from Israel, he occupied himself studying for the Royal College exam. He would lie if he said that he didn't wait for any contact or text from Stephanie. But there wasn't. It made him really sad, especially for the first two months.

He tried to function like normal at work although it was very hard. He really missed Stephanie. He kept thinking about her. Has she recovered well? He wanted to text her first but he already said that he would give her some space. At some point, he was just looking at their pictures together. Although his phone was broken during the explosion, luckily all the photos were backed up in his cloud.

At least studying for the exam helped distract his mind from Stephanie. He had his written exam in March and did his oral exam in May. He thinks they went well. He would be surprised if he didn't pass.

So, this trip to the Rocky Mountains is very important for him. First, is to treat himself after the exams. Second, is to celebrate his thirty-first birthday. Third, is to possibly meet Stephanie again. Although after six months without contact, he is doubtful that she will show up now.

At eleven-fifty a.m., he finally arrives at the summit.

The view takes his breath away for a second. From where he is standing, he can see Lake Louise down below on the right and Lake Agnes down below on the left. But the colors of the lakes are different. Lake Louise has a tulle color while Lake Agnes has a deep blue color. He can also see Big Beehives down below in the middle. In front of him, he can see the opposite mountain ranges. Behind him, there are Mount Niblock and Mount Whyte towering over him. The tops of these mountains are still covered with snow although it is summer.

Stephanie will appreciate this view, for sure. He wishes that he can share this moment with her.

Raphael looks at his surroundings. There are two other couples taking selfies in the summit. There is a group of four older people who seem to enjoy the surroundings. He is the only one by himself. But he is used to it.

At five past twelve, there is still no sign of Stephanie. So, he starts eating his lunch while enjoying the beautiful view.

At twelve-twenty p.m., he finishes his lunch and Stephanie is not there yet. He almost gives up. He will give another fifteen minutes before leaving the summit.

Fifteen minutes later, he stands up and gets ready to leave. His enthusiasm has gone.

Maybe Stephanie's lost memory hasn't recovered yet. Maybe she has forgotten him and is not interested in continuing where they left off. Maybe she is still confused, and booking a plane ticket to Alberta and hiking a challenging mountain for a strange guy is not worth it. After six months without contact, what can he expect? That she will just show up here out of the blue?

But suddenly he hears a familiar voice that he hasn't heard for a while, although he still remembers it clearly.

"Raphael?" someone calls from behind him.

He quickly turns and sees that Stephanie is standing there.

@@@

Stephanie cannot describe how relieved she is when she sees Raphael standing there on the summit of Devil's Thumb. It took a lot of courage for her to book a ticket to Calgary and then travel to Lake Louise and hike up this mountain. And this is for a guy she has had no contact with for the past six months. What if Raphael forgot his promise? But all her worries are gone by the time she sees him now. It looks like he has lost some weight compared to six months ago. But otherwise, he looks healthy and fresh.

She doesn't waste a single second; she runs towards him and hugs him.

Raphael seems shocked at first but he quickly gathers himself and hugs her back.

"Steph! I... I am surprised." Raphael seems to lose his words after they release each other. He looks at her closely. "How are you? How's your recovery?"

"I am good. I have no complaints," she answers.

"Did you get checked thoroughly after you returned to Canada? Did your family doctor refer you to a neurologist and psychiatrist? Did you do rehab? Any side effects after the incident?" Raphael asks worriedly.

"Yes, I have been seeing my neurologist and psychiatrist regularly. I did rehab, too. Everything looks good. No side effects after the incident. How about you?"

"I am good, too. I didn't get injured as badly as you. Only my right shoulder. It doesn't feel the same as before, but it's okay."

"I am glad to hear." She is relieved.

Raphael seems to have a lot of questions for her. But he hesitates a bit. "Have you... recovered your memory?" Raphael finally asks carefully.

"Does it matter?" She looks him in the eyes.

It hasn't been easy for her for the past six months. Even after she returned to Canada, she was still very confused. Everything that happened didn't seem real. She re-read Raphael's letter several times.

Did she really visit North Korea? How come she had no recollection of it? Did she visit Dubai, too? And Raphael did the right thing by telling her through a letter instead of telling her in person. Had he told her in person, she would think that she went crazy. Everything was very overwhelming.

Luckily, although she lost her phone during the incident, all her photos that she took were stored automatically in her cloud. A few days after she returned to Canada, once she finally was able to log in to her cloud, she took the courage to look at these pictures. Initially, a lot of pictures that she took were just the landmarks without her in them. But then, she started to find a lot of pictures of her in North Korea and some selfies with Raphael. There were also pictures with André, Guillaume, Gaby, and Michelle by the swimming pool in Dubai. And some pictures of her skydiving. After that, there were a lot of pictures of her and Raphael hiking in Israel.

It was such a bizarre and scary sensation. Looking at your pictures but having no memory of them. It's like someone else taking over her body for a few weeks. She felt scared. She cried that night because everything was too overwhelming to process.

The appointments with her doctors and therapists were very helpful. When she finally could talk about her concerns to professionals, she felt that the weight in her chest had been lifted up. The doctors and therapists gave her assurance that what she was experiencing was completely normal after a traumatic brain injury.

She played her violin a lot too upon returning to Canada. It helped her feel like herself again. There was a sense of familiarity. However, when she played the first two movements of Dvorak's four romantic pieces, she suddenly felt emotional. She felt an inexplicable mix of joy, hope, as well as thrill. She also felt nostalgic. She was aware that there was something buried in her memory, but she was unable to retrieve it. And that memory was very precious. Then, when she played the last two movements, she remembered what happened in the hospital when she played this piece with André in front of others, including Raphael.

She has also been thinking about Raphael's confession. But because everything was still overwhelming, she decided not to contact him yet. She needed more clarity and more time to think. She tried to remember how she felt towards him, but it was hard. Although the brief moment that they shared in the hospital was very comforting, she didn't want to rush talking to him. She wished that her memories would return first before contacting him.

Around March, she started having recurring dreams about Raphael and others in North Korea, Dubai, and Israel. She thought it was because she kept reading Raphael's letter and kept looking at her pictures and tried to re-construct what happened. She was not sure if these were her imagination or they were actually her real memories. Sometimes she had some flashbacks and felt nostalgic about certain things, like the colorful buildings in North Korea, the gigantic and luxurious buildings in the middle of the desert in Dubai, and the Galilean landscape in Israel. However, she didn't know if these things were in her mind because she had researched them or it was because she had truly seen and experienced them. How could she tell?

Sometimes when she imagined Raphael's face, she felt warm in her body but followed by hollowness. It was like she missed something precious in her life. She missed him. Her dreams and her imaginations about him made her think about him every day since the past few months. If her imaginations are not just imaginations but real, she understands why she fell in love with him. But what if her imaginations about him are different from reality? How could she tell?

That's why she is here now.

Sooner or later, she has to know what actually happened. She wants to know which ones are her imaginations and which ones are her real memories. She wants to know the real Raphael.

"Does it really matter if I remember everything or not?" Stephanie repeats her question as Raphael seems to be confused by her reply.

"That is only to determine what I should say to you and what I should not. But regardless, I still want to love you, Steph." Raphael looks deeply into her eyes.

She feels touched and relieved at the same time. Throughout this time, she is not sure if she deserves to have Raphael without her memory.

"Thanks, Raphael." She hugs him again. It feels like a dream to hug him like this. Although she hasn't confirmed if Raphael is really like what she has imagined or not. But his warmth, his scent, and his embrace all feel very familiar.

"The truth is, I think I have some ideas about what actually happened between us six months ago. But that's because I have seen pictures. After that, I started to have dreams and started imagining things. And how would I know which ones are real and which ones are my imaginations?"

"You can always ask me. But that can wait. Let's enjoy this beautiful view first, and then we can chat further on the way down. Sounds good?" Raphael asks. Stephanie is glad to hear this. That means that even without her memory, he still loves her!

"Yes," she replies. "And by the way, happy birthday."

He kisses her forehead as a 'thank you' gesture and they enjoy the beautiful view.

@@@

The past few hours seem unreal to Raphael. He still cannot believe that Stephanie is standing next to him and talking to him. They hiked down together and now they are enjoying a nice drink in the Lakeview Lounge at Fairmont Chateau Lake Louise. The restaurant has giant windows that offer the beautiful view of the lake. They sit by the window to enjoy the view.

"And this one is a bit embarrassing..." Stephanie appears hesitant. On the way down, she told him what she thought was happening and asked for his confirmation. Raphael found this activity really fun. Most of the time, Stephanie actually described real events, not just her imagination. She remembered the first time they met in the ER; he stitched her wounds and was skeptical about her profession as a music therapist. Now it has become a sweet memory for him. She remembered they played squash with Guillaume and went to André's place at Shangri-La. That's where Raphael decided to go to North Korea with her. She remembered they met new people in North Korea, although she didn't remember the names, like Brad and Lindsay. But she was able to describe their physical appearance. It appears that she truly has regained some of her memories because Raphael never told her this detail and there were no pictures of these events.

"That's okay. Tell me." Raphael is curious what she is about to ask.

"I... did we meet Kim Jong-Un in North Korea? This must be only my imagination, right?" She seems very doubtful, which he can understand.

"First, tell me more. What did you dream or imagine about Kim Jong-Un?" Throughout this interview, Raphael usually only says yes or no. He doesn't want to give further information voluntarily.

"That I played violin for him. And you were there among the audience."

"What did you play?"

Stephanie seems to be thinking hard. "I played so many violin pieces in my life. I can't remember, sorry."

"That's okay." Raphael feels a slight disappointment. The music that she played had left a deep impression on him. But he reminds himself that he is supposed to be grateful that she has recovered some of her memory. It's very normal that she doesn't remember some.

Stephanie also remembers some events in Dubai, such as when she worked out with Guillaume and went swimming with André. She also remembers when they went skydiving but she didn't count it as recovered memory because she has seen the pictures before having a memory of it.

"And I vaguely remember that you fell into the swimming pool."

Raphael's eyes widen. "And then what happened?"

"I remember André and I were also in the swimming pool. Did we save you by any chance?"

"Yes, you guys did. What happened after?"

"I remember you had a bad dream that night, and then you threw up."

Raphael nods. Before, he was embarrassed about this. But now he doesn't care. He is even happy that Stephanie remembers this.

"I also remember Gaby and Michelle did a makeover on me and André asked me to play the violin for you."

"Do you remember what you played?"

Stephanie shakes her head again. "No, sorry."

Raphael puts his hand over hers. "It's okay, Steph."

"After that, we visited Jerusalem, Dead Sea, and we did the same hike as the one I did a couple years ago. But again, I first knew this because I saw our pictures."

"Did you remember any of our conversations in Jerusalem by any chance?"

Stephanie suddenly looks a bit shy and hesitant.

"Did you say you love me when we were in Mount Olives in Jerusalem?" Stephanie looks at her lap when saying it. "I hope I didn't imagine things," she continues.

"You didn't."

She raises her head and looks at him. Now she becomes more confident in her memory, which is what he wants.

"And I replied back to you after we went swimming in the Dead Sea, right?" she asks.

"Yes. You said that you love me. I hope it is still the case now."

"It is."

Chapter 28

Early June
Banff, Alberta

From Lake Louise, they return to Banff at around five p.m. Stephanie has booked a hotel room in downtown Banff while Raphael booked a room at Fairmont Banff Springs. Since the distance is about thirty minutes' walk, Raphael proposes that she stays at his place tonight.

Once they arrive at Fairmont Banff Springs, André, Guillaume, Gaby, and Michelle have arrived there to welcome them.

"Stephanie! It's good to see you here." Gaby quickly hugs her. André, Guillaume, and Michelle also give her warm hugs. After that, they have dinner at one of the restaurants in the hotel to catch up. Once they place their order, Stephanie confirms some of her memories with them.

"You got pretty much everything right," Guillaume said while cutting his steak. Stephanie has just recounted what she thought was happening in Dubai.

"I am glad that you finally recall the favor that you did for me. I started swimming and playing piano again," André says.

Stephanie drinks her water before replying. "Yeah, but unfortunately I don't remember the piece that I played when we gathered in the living room."

After everybody finishes eating, Gaby suddenly says, "I have an idea."

Now everybody is looking at Gaby. She gets up, walks towards Raphael, and whispers into his ear. He seems to be hesitant.

"What's going on?" Stephanie asks.

"It's a surprise," Gaby replies. "Michelle, Guillaume, how about you take Stephanie to Rundle Bar and we will meet you there?"

Guillaume and Michelle nod and they lead Stephanie upstairs to the mezzanine level. The bar is very beautiful and it has a piano. The lighting is dim and it makes the atmosphere more intimate. There is also a terrace where people can enjoy the view of surrounding mountains.

A few minutes later, Raphael, Gaby, and André arrive. And Raphael is carrying a violin!

But instead of giving the violin to her, he opens the violin case himself and starts tuning it with Gaby's help on the piano.

André, Guillaume, Michelle, and Stephanie take a seat close to the piano.

After that, Raphael and Gaby start their duet. Raphael is playing the violin and Gaby is playing the piano.

They play Dvorak's four romantic pieces.

The beautiful melody of the first movement—Allegro Moderato (Cavatina)—starts filling her ears and her heart. She feels the warmth and the familiarity. But wait, since when can Raphael play violin? He is sliding the bow across the strings confidently and steadily. He also looks very emotional and immersed in his music. The female audience in the room can't take their eyes off him. He looks very handsome and skillful when standing there, playing his violin. Stephanie never had any memory of him playing the violin like this. She feels disappointed that she didn't recover this part of her memory.

Suddenly she has a flashback of her playing the violin in North Korea. She remembers the room, the people there, Kim Jong-Un in the front, and Raphael at the back. She remembers the dress that she wore as well. This must be it! This must be the song that she played at that time. It's weird that she has played this piece several times for the past six months, but she didn't have this flashback. But when Raphael plays it, she starts to remember.

Maybe because she usually played this piece with different interpretations depending on her mood. Maybe the way Raphael plays it now is similar to the way she played it back in North Korea.

She feels the calmness generated by the music. In the middle, she feels the intensity. Just like what she experienced in North Korea when she thought they were going to capture her. But then, Raphael closes the piece gently and beautifully.

She is very impressed.

After that, the second movement—Allegro Maestoso (Capriccio)—begins.

The music brings back her memories in Dubai. She remembers she went skydiving with Raphael. It was definitely thrilling like this song. But it was also fun. Then she remembers the fight Raphael got into and when he almost drowned in the swimming pool. She was scared that he would get injured. But luckily in the end, he was okay. Listening to this piece makes the memories in her head clearer.

She suddenly remembers performing in a lobby hotel in Dubai with André. She was wearing a blue dress. Another puzzle is solved. This must be the piece she played to console Raphael after he had a traumatic experience.

Now the third movement—Allegro Appassionato (Romance)—begins.

She is aware that she played this piece when they were in the hospital in Tel Aviv. This melody reminds her of the peaceful Galilean landscape that they enjoyed during the hike. Now this image in her head becomes more vivid. Before, it was like she was the third person observing two new lovers going on a hike. But now she knows that it's herself that she was observing and Raphael is the lover. She clearly remembers how they were struggling in the rain but at the end they managed to complete the hike that brought them closer than before.

Finally, the fourth and longest movement—Larghetto (Elegy)—begins.

This piece is such a sad piece. It embodies tragedy, heartbreak, and loss. This must be how Raphael felt when he discovered that she lost her memory and didn't remember him. She remembers how sad he looked when they were in the hospital. This piece is also representative of how she felt after she returned to Canada and was recovering from her injuries. She felt unfamiliar and empty even when she was in a familiar environment in Toronto with her family. She felt like she had lost something precious.

After Raphael finishes, they all give him standing applause. Not only them, but also other guests in the bar seem to enjoy his music.

When Raphael walks towards her, she cannot stop herself. She hugs him and whispers in his ears.

"That's very beautiful, Raphael."

"Thank you. Do you like it?"

"Yes. Now I remember, the first movement was the one I played in North Korea, right? And the second movement was the one I played in Dubai?" she confirms with him.

Raphael nods his head enthusiastically. "Yes! I am glad that you finally remember."

"However, since when did you play violin? I didn't remember you playing during our trip."

"Well... You remembered it correctly. I didn't play during our trip. In fact, I had never played violin until six months ago," Raphael explains.

Her jaw drops. What? But he has just played the violin effortlessly like he has been playing for quite a while. Stephanie can tell that he is not a professional, sometimes the tempo is a bit off, but Raphael was so confident to the point that people thought that he did it on purpose.

"Wow. You decided to start playing violin because..."

"Because of you, yes. After I returned to Canada, I missed you so much. I wanted to feel closer to you. I wanted to replay our trip and these pieces reminded me of it. These are the only pieces that I can play."

She laughs at his confession. She finds Raphael very honest and adorable.

"Now it's your turn," Raphael continues.

"My turn?"

"To play, yes. Can I request a song?"

"What is it?"

"Your composition, 'Epinephrine'."

Oh, how did he know that she composed a song? She must have shown him although she did not remember.

"Sure." She receives the violin that Raphael hands her. She notices that there are four marks on the fingerboard. Now she knows how Raphael could produce an almost perfect pitch throughout his performance. But she finds his 'cheating' method cute.

She walks onto the stage and faces the audience. Although there are other people watching her, in her mind, she is playing this for Raphael as well as André, Gaby, Guillaume, and Michelle.

Then she starts playing.

While she is playing, she starts imagining herself on adventures again with Raphael. It was fun and thrilling. Also, now she remembers that she played this song in their hotel suite in Dubai. In addition to triggering nostalgia, music really opens people's mind, imagination, as well as enhancing past memories.

Once she finishes Epinephrine, people give her a big applause. Then, André approaches her with a music sheet in his hand.

"Do you remember this piece, Steph?" He asks.

She reads the title, it says 'Dopamine'. It doesn't mean anything to her until she reads the music sheet and tries to play the melody in her head.

"Somehow, this music is familiar."

"Wanna give it a try?"

"Sure."

Although the music is a virtuosic piece with allegro tempo, it doesn't look very hard. And she is right. Once she starts playing it, it feels natural to her, like she has played it before. She has the muscle memory for this piece.

Then she remembers that this was the piece she played with André in the hotel lobby in Dubai to console Raphael. This was the piece that she played after playing Capriccio, the second movement of the Four Romantic Pieces. Another memory is triggered.

This piece really describes her relationship with Raphael. Very fast-paced, sweet at the same time, but most importantly, very rewarding.

After she finishes the piece, she turns towards André on the piano.

"Now I remember, isn't this your composition?" she asks.

André nods. "Yes. The one I composed after listening to your 'Epinephrine'. I realized that I hadn't composed any music for a while. And when I started again, I felt like I accomplished something."

If André was her client, this is the most rewarding thing that a music therapist can experience. When a client manages to compose music and feels an improvement in their lives. Whether it's an improvement to express their emotion, communication skills, or even self-esteem.

Raphael walks towards them. "Also, André said that our relationship was the inspiration for the piece that you have just played." He smiles proudly.

"Wow, I feel honored," she says.

André turns to Raphael. "Hey, Raphael. Now it's your turn to play the last piece." He looks at Raphael meaningfully.

Stephanie doesn't follow. What other pieces didn't she remember?

Raphael seems to understand. So, she gives the violin back to Raphael and sits with Gaby, Guillaume, and Michelle in the audience.

Then, Raphael starts playing a song that she has never heard before. The melody is simple but full of joy and passion. It makes her imagine two people who fall in love deeply with one another. Not just passion, but also bonding, attachment, and trust. This piece feels fresh and uplifting for the mood.

When Raphael finishes, Guillaume, Michelle, Gaby and she give a standing applause.

Raphael bows and walks towards her. "How do you like the piece? Do you have any feedback?"

"Wait, is it you who composed this piece?" Stephanie asks Raphael in disbelief.

Raphael nods shyly. "I know it's far from perfect. It's my first time. Of course, André and Gaby helped, but..."

"Raphael." She cuts him off. He looks at her. "It was perfect. I mean it." She looks him straight in the eyes. She is very impressed that Raphael, who didn't play violin until six months ago, could also compose such a beautiful piece.

"Thank you," Raphael says. "Can you guess the name of the piece?"

She can only think of one word.

"Oxytocin."

@@@

Raphael is enjoying his drink on the balcony from his hotel room that night. He can see the lights from downtown Banff below.

Tonight is one of the best birthdays he has ever had. After six months learning violin, he can finally perform it in front of Stephanie. When he was packing for the trip, he wasn't sure if he should bring the violin as Stephanie may not be here. But he decided to bring it anyway, just in case. Luckily Stephanie showed up and he could help her regain her memory by playing the pieces that meant something for her.

He never considers himself a musical person. But the fact that Stephanie lost her memory and didn't contact him after they returned to Canada hurt him a lot. He needed something to console himself. He needed music therapy. That's why he decided to start learning violin. He heard that people cannot learn classical piano as an adult, but for classical violin, it's possible. He recalls his friends and sisters' reaction when he told them his intention.

"You want to do what?" André asked him in disbelief when they gathered at Shangri-La one night six months ago.

"I want to learn how to play the violin," he replied confidently. Nobody asked the reason because they all already knew.

"Aren't you too old for that?" Guillaume asked.

"Learning is a lifetime process." He shrugged. "Look, I just want to learn Dvorak's Four Romantic Pieces. That's all. It shouldn't be too bad, right?"

Nobody said anything at first. But finally, André asked, "Okay, can you read music sheets?"

"Not really. I learned some when I was little, but I have forgotten all of them now."

Gaby jumps in. "I will help you, Raphael. I believe in you." Raphael looked at her full of gratitude. Gaby has always been his biggest supporter.

"And what is your timeline for mastering these pieces?" Michelle asked.

"Umm... six months?"

Nobody said anything for a while. Everybody was just looking at him with pity. He knew what they thought. It was an impossible mission.

But regardless, after that meeting, in the midst of his brutal shifts and exam preparation, he practiced the violin diligently. In a way, keeping himself busy was the only way he could distract himself from the sadness. Luckily, André and Gaby understood that and they helped him tremendously. At one point, he almost gave up, especially when realizing how complicated the second movement was. He even hadn't mastered the first movement well.

"C'mon, Raphael, you can do this. Maybe just memorize the melody if reading the music sheet is too hard," André advised.

"And, don't rush. Play it slow first," Gaby added.

Finally, after a few months, he started making progress and his playing started to become more enjoyable. Even André and Gaby were impressed with his determination. At some point, he also asked them to show him how to compose music. He hummed the melody while André was transcribing on the sheet music so that he didn't forget the melody.

Around May, he finally was able to play all four movements of the romantic pieces plus his own composition that he called 'Oxytocin'. He wasn't playing like a professional, but who cares. At least André told him that he played extremely well for someone who had just started violin five months ago.

Finally, today, he could perform the pieces he learned and he composed in front of Stephanie. He was aware that he made some awkward errors but he kept going and didn't stop when that happened. He focused on the melody and the emotion, and less on the technical details. He just wanted to make Stephanie happy.

Suddenly a noise behind him brings him back from his lamentation to the present.

Stephanie has just finished taking a shower and her hair is still wet. She is wearing her pajamas with a towel around her neck.

Although she is fully clothed, Raphael finds her very...sexy. Raphael likes the fact that she is more on the shy spectrum and not trying to seduce him like other girls.

"Hey." She approaches him to the balcony.

"Hey."

"I am still thinking about your performance. How beautiful it was. And the more I replay it in my head, the clearer my memories are," she says.

"I am glad. But again, my feelings towards you will still be the same regardless of how vivid your memory is."

"Thanks." She gives him a quick kiss on the cheek. He likes when she does that!

Now he feels like he cannot restrain himself anymore. He kisses her passionately on the lips and she kisses him back. They move to the bed together while still kissing each other.

He puts her on the bed gently. But then he is curious about something.

"Tell me, do you remember something similar to this in the past?"

Stephanie looks at him "Umm.. yes. In Israel, in Cana..." Now she looks unsure.

"What do you remember?" He gives her a naughty look.

"I don't remember we did it, but I remember how I really enjoyed your touch and how I really admired... your body. Was it just my imagination?" She looks at him shyly.

He continues kissing her. "Let's find out."

Chapter 29

Early June
Banff, Alberta

Raphael and Stephanie almost arrive at the summit of Sulphur Mountain. They have been hiking this mountain for the past two hours. As usual, André, Guillaume, Gaby, and Michelle prefer to ride the gondola instead of hiking.

Once they arrive at the summit, his friends and sisters are already there. They eat lunch together at the restaurant at the summit. Raphael still cannot believe his good luck that Stephanie is back and there are six of them again instead of just five. He cannot stop smiling to himself.

They admire the view of Banff and surrounding mountains from the summit for a while.

"Thanks for coming back to my side, Steph," he says to Stephanie while holding her hands.

She squeezes his hand back. "Thanks for waiting for me."

"You know, before I met you, I didn't realize what I was missing in life. I am grateful that you were willing to accompany me hiking this morning, even though we can take the gondola. As much as I love my friends and my sisters, I have to accept that they are not as adventurous as me. If you weren't here, I would have hiked by myself and it wouldn't be as fun as if it were with someone." He kisses the back of her hand.

"I feel the same. I have never found someone who is as adventurous as me until I met you. Thanks for coming into my life. I look forward to sharing more adventures together." She smiles. Raphael never feels this happy, light, and fulfilled in his life.

When they are about to go down, Michelle insists that they go down together with a gondola so that they can take pictures together. Stephanie and he have no choice but to agree. But he doesn't regret it because the view from the gondola is gorgeous, too. And they can do more activities when they return to the village because they have saved time taking the gondola down instead of hiking.

André and Gaby decide to enjoy the hot spring near the gondola station. Guillaume and Michelle decide to go shopping in downtown Banff. Raphael and Stephanie decide to just take a walk along the trails by the Bow River.

In the middle of walking, they see a beautiful white gazebo and decide to take a look. Raphael really likes this discovery. The gazebo with mountain background really gives the European Swiss Alps vibe, although they are in Canada.

They sit in the gazebo while enjoying their surroundings.

Stephanie opens a conversation. "You know, on the way to Alberta, I still had a lot of uncertainties about us because I couldn't trust my memory yet. But now that everything has been confirmed, can you imagine how relieved and happy I am? The things I have been imagining turn out to be real! Our love is real! Once we return to Canada, I am not going to hold myself back like before." He can hear more conviction in her voice which makes him very happy, too.

"Yes please, don't hold back. I am not going to hold myself back anymore either."

"I don't care if it's all happening too fast. I am certain about how I feel and I know that I want to be with you," she says.

"I think this is how we are, we are used to a fast-paced environment. Fast-paced adventure, fast-paced music, and fast-paced romance. Your composition 'Epinephrine' is a fast-paced adventurous feeling. André's composition for us, 'Dopamine', is a fast-paced relationship that leads to rewarding experience. And my composition 'Oxytocin' is a fast-paced passion between us. However, what I was trying to convey through my composition is this passion between us; although it comes fast, it is long-lasting.

It's followed by a long-term commitment. It creates trust. I really see my future with you."

"Me, too. Every time I replay these three compositions in my head, I think about how beautiful our fast-paced romance is. I also see a future with you, that's why I don't want it to end," Stephanie says.

"Do you know what we should call these three movements of violin composition?" Raphael asks.

"What?"

"Romance Allegro."

-Fin-

About the Author

Nydia was born in Jakarta, Indonesia, and moved to Canada when she was 18 years old. In 2017, she graduated from the University of Alberta in Edmonton, then moved to Calgary, Toronto, and finally to Montreal in 2021. Living in various cities in Canada has broadened her perspective as a Canadian author.

During her spare time, she enjoys reading, writing, playing piano, and making videos for her YouTube channel, Nyds Learning French.

The inspiration for her writing includes: Montreal and Canada's beauty, her Asian roots, classical music, her travel experience, and her faith and spirituality.

AOS Publications:
Romance Concerto (2024)
Romance Allegro (2025)

For more information, visit www.nydiahadi.com